SLAY AND SLAY AGAIN!

An anthology of queer horror

Edited by Ben Walker

"Queer horror is having a moment, even as legislation seeks to erase queer people and suppress our voices. While some respond with increasing self-censure and polite deferment, the authors in *Slay And Slay Again* refuse to hide or apologize for who they are. Their stories reflect the rich variety of the darker side of queer human experience, the sick and delightful desires of explorers who challenge mental and sexual boundaries, the drama of discovering identity, and the pains and passions of bodies that will only be tamed by authenticity." - Joe Koch, author of *The Wingspan of Severed Hands* and *Invaginies*

This edition first published 2024 – also available as an ebook

Paperback ISBN: 9798323406371

Web: slicedupress.com / Bluesky: slicedupress.bsky.social
Tumblr: tumblr.com/slicedupress

Cover art courtesy of DepositPhotos/grandeduc (Jukka Nieminen)

CONTENTS

CAREFUL MAKING WISHES IN THE DARK

Eva Roslin

The sorceress, with jealous rage
Sewed me up between my legs
Tight stitches, burning weeds
She closed me up
Left a husk behind
A punishment
Half a woman
Why, I don't know
My heart trailed after others it knew I could not have
Affections that belonged only to others
Girls who rested their heads on lovers' chests
Whose flesh opened and bloomed,
Wide, accommodating,
Slick.

With each heart that I longed for,
threads tight
bound,
sealed.
Every moment, an agony
Wires pulling, burning me like vilest acid
dripping red wax
forcing me to wonder
if my flesh will ever open again.

THE BIRTHDAY HOLE

Eric Raglin

Vanilla sex satisfied Ben at first, but it did nothing for him after a while. Three months in, while I was sucking his cock, he got this faraway look in his eyes, probably imagining much filthier scenes. My swirling tongue couldn't compete with his fantasies, which I'm convinced were the only thing keeping him hard.

I'd fucked a dozen men before Ben and never had this problem. My lovers had all moaned and writhed and run their fingers through my hair when I blew them, begging me to keep going even when I felt five seconds away from lockjaw.

Was I using too much teeth? Had I become ugly the day I turned thirty? I didn't know. But accepting that I couldn't satisfy Ben was out of the question. He was every self-hating gay man's dream: straight-passing in both appearance and behavior, his muscles bulging, his voice deep, and his interests outside the realm of pop divas and Drag Race. The type of hunk I'd imagined while jerking off from age twelve onward. If I wanted to keep him, I'd just have to get creative the next time we fucked—so long as he didn't ghost me first.

Thankfully, he agreed to meet up again and suggested a cafe. The location disappointed me, having neither the neon sex appeal of a nightclub nor the rugged eroticism of a hiking trail. You only took someone to a cafe if you wanted to break up with them. The environment was too sober and relaxed for heartbroken screaming matches—only civil partings.

This cafe was full of college students cramming for finals and Bible study groups deep in sacred discussions. Ben sat at a corner table by the restrooms, leaning back in his chair and scrolling through his phone. When he saw me, he nodded in a straight guy kind of way that melted my heart, then returned to his phone to finish texting someone. I sat across from him.

"Can I buy you a coffee?" I asked.

"Nah, I'm good," he said. "Keeyan, I actually wanted to talk about something. I don't really think we're—"

The restroom door opened, and a woman wearing a rosary smiled too widely at Ben as she squeezed past him. "Ope, sorry," she said. "Tight quarters."

Right then, I knew how to stop Ben from breaking up with me.

Leaning across the table, I whispered, "I have an idea."

Ben closed his eyes as if my voice—no matter how quiet—gave him a migraine. "Listen," he said. "I don't want to be rude, but—"

"Take me into that restroom and cum on my face."

My words came out too loud, too desperate. I worried one of the Bible groups had heard me, but they were too busy discussing the sins of the Canaanites to condemn the sins happening one table over.

Ben gawked as if I'd just emerged from a cocoon, my hot slut metamorphosis complete. He pulled me into the restroom like I was his dog on a leash, not seeming to care if anyone noticed. Maybe he wanted them to see—to make them go quiet after the lock clicked, listening for the muffled slaps of flesh against flesh. When we emerged, sweaty and grinning, would the Christians be gone, scandalized into retreat? Would the cops be waiting in their place?

I'm sure these possibilities aroused Ben more than scared him, but for me, it was the opposite. I didn't want to cause a scene or wind up in jail. I just wanted to keep my boyfriend interested.

Within seconds of locking the door, Ben unzipped his pants, forced me to the sticky tile floor, and shoved his cock down my throat. Grasping fistfuls of my hair, he facefucked me hard, then pulled out, shooting hot syrupy ropes across my face. He'd lasted thirty seconds, max. But, seeing his dizzy-eyed smile, I could tell they'd been the best thirty seconds of his life.

* * *

Upping the ante to keep Ben from breaking up with me was fun at first, and I spent hours dreaming up new ways to satisfy him. Porn provided plenty of inspiration. We tried everything from choking to watersports. I didn't like the bruises around my neck or the tang of too-dark piss on my tongue, but I loved how Ben looked while doing these things to me—his ice-blue eyes almost feral with pleasure. He was like a dumb, animalistic frat boy with hormones potent enough to fuel the world's largest orgy. No man had ever been so perfect for me. I imagined showing him off to my family like a prize stallion. *Wow*, my dad would say. *Finally, a man's man! No more sissies, huh?* Too bad Ben had no interest in meeting my parents.

Whenever I stayed the night at his place, I'd wake up the next morning too hungover to think, so I'd shuffle into the kitchen and ask him what vile thing he wanted to try next. He only ever shrugged, then returned to whatever he was doing—cooking up eggs and bacon for one or listening to some edgy comedy podcast. I could never tell if he was too lazy to brainstorm or if he just liked being surprised.

By necessity, my ideas became more extreme. One night, I soaked in an ice bath for ten minutes to prepare for simulated necrophilia. While I lay death-still in his bed, Ben rolled on a condom, shoved his dick inside me, and moaned, "Fuck, that corpse bussy is so cold and tight." It took all my power to hold back a snort, but at least the experience was more funny than disturbing.

The same couldn't be said for what I planned the next night. I led Ben in a bugchaser roleplay, pretending he had HIV and begging him to cum deep in my ass. Going bareback for the first time, he thrusted with seizure-like rhythm and intensity, saying he'd fill me "full of fuckin' AIDS, you disease-loving slut." Soon, he was frothing at the mouth, drooling across my neck and chest as his grunted promises—threats?—became less and less coherent. While our necrophilia roleplay had felt safely distant from reality, this experience—with his raw cock grinding against my rectum and his mouth hissing violence—felt far too real. I was closing up, reaching my limits of depravity. Unable to take any more, I grabbed his arm.

"I—I think this scene is too much for me," I said.

He stopped pumping and glared with wide, insane eyes. His face was red and bulging as if his cum had backed up all the way into his skull and would explode outward at any moment. "Are you kidding? It was *your* idea."

I thought about saying "Never mind, you're right" and just letting him have this one, but I had to trust my gut. "Yeah, no, I'm really not into it."

I scooted my ass away from him, and his dick slipped out, already half-soft.

"Fine," he said through gritted teeth. With sharp, violent movements, he snatched a ratty bath towel from the floor and wiped cloudy gobs of lube off his dick. "You should leave."

My heart sank. He'd been looking forward to this fucked-up little roleplay, and I'd had the audacity to blueball him—not even in a sexual way! Sure, I'd respected my own limits, but at what cost?

Ben told me to get dressed. I did so quickly and silently, but before I had a chance to tie my shoes, he pushed me out the door and slammed it behind me.

I didn't sleep that night, and instead stayed up wondering how I could win Ben back. I'd have to lure him in with a sexual act so wretched that he'd be unable to resist. But the more I researched and the harder I thought, the more convinced I became that no such act existed. At least not one I felt comfortable with.

The next morning, I tried texting him, *Hey, sorry about last night. Can we talk?*, but the message didn't go through; I was blocked.

The hottest guy I'd ever dated—the only one who even my dad would approve of—wanted nothing to do with me.

* * *

Ben's birthday was one day away. I found out from his Facebook, the only app he hadn't blocked me on. After all, why bother when he hadn't posted there in years?

I thought about the type of sex he'd want on his birthday. Something so intense and depraved I'd have to take the next day off to recover, both physically and spiritually. Maybe I'd never be able to give him that.

If only Ben were easier to please. I thought back to my college boyfriend RJ who would've been happy with basic, no-frills blowjobs for the rest of his life. He'd only ever fucked me in the ass once, the day he turned nineteen. *The birthday hole*, he'd called it, and we'd both laughed.

As soon as I remembered that phrase, something stirred in me. Those words repeated in my head like a hypnotic mantra: *the birthday hole ... the birthday hole*. At first, I figured it was like a dumb pop song stuck in a mental loop, but time would prove me wrong.

The next evolution of the birthday hole was

coming.

* * *

That night, my dreams boiled into malformed visions.

A callused tunnel contracting.

Lightyears of oozing cosmic muscle.

The tang of shit.

The tingle of mint.

The smack and squelch of Something dragging itself through jellied wastes.

Glistening, starless darkness.

A sob swallowing a laugh swallowing a moan.

I woke up soaked in sweat, my sheets twisted into a wet whip. My whole bed was sopping, and I wondered if I'd pissed myself. It had happened to me once or twice in my blackout-drunk early twenties, but this time I'd only had a couple beers before bed.

Something tickled my chest, then dripped onto the bed. Looking down, I discovered the truth. I hadn't pissed myself or sweated out a week's worth of liquid. No, something was leaking from an opening just above my heart. The cut was the size and shape of an almond, exposing pink pec muscle. The dripping liquid wasn't blood though; it was gray and translucent, like big city slush. My formerly cream-colored sheets had taken on the same joyless hue.

I swiped my finger through the fluid and sniffed it. Maybe my dreams had infected my imagination, but I swore I smelled shit and mint. The scents disappeared in an instant, as if deciding I was unworthy to smell them. They would only return for the right person. The thought was insane, but I somehow knew it was true. This hole was a gift for Ben. And if it could bring him back into my life, it would be a gift to me, too.

The hole got bigger throughout the day. Whenever it widened, it felt like my flesh was yawning. Soon the hole grew to the size of a fist, the sheen of its pink lining exposed to open air. I fingered it to see how it felt, but it contracted, squeezing until I thought my bones would break. It was the hole's way of saying, *Not for you.*

Unable to reach Ben any other way, I drove to his apartment. Outside his door, I could hear him talking with someone—another man with a voice higher and shriller than my own. Ben had already replaced me with the perfect twink to dominate, humiliate, and dispose of after he'd outlived his novelty. A lump rose in my throat.

But I couldn't stop here. The hole pulsed and stretched, beckoning Ben from beyond the door. I hesitated only a moment longer, then knocked.

"That's probably the pizza," the twink said on the other side.

"We already ate," Ben said. "I'm not paying for that."

"Oh, I know. We're not eating it. You're going to shove each and every slice up my ass. Fill me up until my fucking colon bursts."

Ben let out something halfway between a laugh and a low, horny growl. "Well, I've never tried that before. Go get it."

When the twink opened the door, I was too stunned to speak. I'd never be able to compete with this cute twig-of-a-man's bizarre erotic ingenuity.

Maybe he'd have enough perverse ideas—and few enough reservations—for Ben to keep him around. Maybe the twink even enjoyed trying those ideas out—not for Ben's pleasure, but his own. For a long moment, we just stared at each other. Finally, he blinked his long eyelashes and broke the silence.

"Um, can I help you?"

"Yeah, I, uh—" The hole squelched out a glob of mucus that trailed down my stomach. "Can I talk to Ben?"

He glared at me, then called to Ben. "Babe, there's some weird guy at the door for you."

"Who are you talking about?" Ben asked from some unseen corner of the apartment. "I know a lot of weird guys, and some of them never leave me the fuck alone."

A barb of pain shot through my heart, but I tried not to show it. I put on the most casual expression I could muster—a face that couldn't possibly belong to a "weird guy". The hole squeezed out another glob of something. It smelled sharp, like mustard, and seeped through my shirt, all too visible now. I regretted not wearing a darker color.

"Is that sweat or are you—?"

Ben appeared in the doorway before the twink could finish his question. The second he saw me, a chill descended.

"Why are you here, Keeyan?" he asked, then turned to the twink. "Wait, Carter, did you set this up? Threesomes are boring. Literally the most basic shit."

"I didn't—"

Again, the twink didn't get two words in before I ripped my shirt off, the mustard-smelling goo smearing across my chin in the process. It felt like Icy-Hot on my skin, burning one moment and freezing the next. Whatever it was didn't matter. I had to show Ben.

"This is yours," I said, pointing to the hole. "It's your birthday, right? I—I wanted to make sure it was special."

Carter's eyes went wide as large pizzas, then he fled to the bathroom and retched chunks into the toilet.

Ben just stared at the hole, cocking his head like a dog.

"What is it?" he finally asked.

"I have no fucking clue," I said, stepping inside and closing the door. "But I want you to try it."

"Okay."

While stripping, he never once blinked or looked away. He didn't bite his lip or drool or make rabid grizzly bear horndog sounds. I think whatever arousal he felt couldn't be expressed in his usual ways; this turn-on was more cosmic than physical.

Hypnotized, he approached me and, without hesitation, balled up his fist and pressed it against the hole's sticky pink rim. The hole pulsed, secreting a lubricating froth that looked like soap bubbles with a mucusy sheen. Ben pushed his fist inside. His fingers were right where my heart should have been, but I felt nothing; this experience wasn't about me. He sank deeper, all the way to his elbow. His jaw fell open, trembling uncontrollably.

"Yeah, you like that?" I asked, because what else was I going to say? But Ben didn't react to my words. I wanted him to acknowledge me. "I grew this thing just for you. I'd do anything for—"

He slapped a hand over my mouth. "Shuuuuuuut theeeee fuuuuuuuuuuck uuuuuuup," he said, pleasure or pain or sensation beyond description drawing out his syllables like a stiff electric current.

Gripping the edge of the hole with his other hand, he pulled. It stretched to his whims, its elasticity sentient and submissive. Still, I felt nothing. Not the tearing of skin and muscle, nor the sensation of organs smashing against my ribcage to make room for the star of the show.

Two muscular arms shoved inside me.

A thick head.

The shoulders of a linebacker.

I dissociated, the squelch of his entry turning to a static lullaby.

Distantly, I registered Carter returning to the room, his muffled scream, the terror and fascination in his eyes. I registered Ben's hairy feet doing almost a mermaid kick in the air, then disappearing inside me—inside *it*.

Then … *SCHLOP*!

The sound of the hole closing snapped me back to reality. Panicking, I ran both my hands over my chest, trying to find where the hole had gone. Was there a button, a knob to open it back up? But the longer I searched, the more certain I became; the hole wasn't going to reopen. Ben was gone, trapped somewhere both impossible and irresistible.

* * *

Dating Carter after the hole swallowed Ben was

fucked up, but shared trauma bonds people in strange ways. It wasn't like we could tell anyone our secret. We could only process those feelings with each other—sometimes through words, but more often through touch.

"That bitch was insatiable," Carter told me one night in the sweaty afterglow of sex. "He was hot, and I felt lucky that he even looked at me. But goddamn, I don't think I could've satisfied him for much longer."

Hearing Carter voice the idea I'd thought many times but never put into words got me teary.

"Thank you," I said. "For not being like him."

But Carter wasn't like my college boyfriend either. He enjoyed a good meat-and-potatoes blowjob, of course, but he liked experimenting, too. Thankfully, our experiments—some bondage here, a little puppy play there—kept his interest beyond just the first try. I didn't have to be his personal novelty dispenser. Ben might have been more my type physically—and certainly the more strong-wristed, father-approved option—but Carter was a much better match for me in the long run.

While grief and guilt often colored our relationship, the next six months were mostly blissful. Our connection even extended beyond the bedroom. We discovered our mutual interest in performance art, John Waters movies, and competitive figure skating, and could talk for hours about these topics, laughing and gasping and gabbing away the night. Our bond felt rare and special, like something destined to last.

Then came Carter's birthday.

I woke up beside him that morning with something wet and sticky on my chest, still covered with a sheet. At first, I thought it was my cum from the night before, somehow not yet dried, but the moist area was too large to have come from my load alone. Unfortunately, Carter had been too drunk—or distracted, tired, *something*—to contribute his own. He never even got hard, but not for lack of trying. In the dinner plate-sized wet spot, the sheets dipped a couple inches as if my chest had caved in.

I knew right then that the hole had returned. Nausea rippled through my stomach—wherever that organ had been temporarily displaced to.

Before I could wake Carter, the sheet lifted slightly. Four small wormlike shapes rose and tickled the navy fabric from below. Frozen, I watched as they shifted back and forth in a hypnotic rhythm. I realized these weren't wriggling worms; they were waving fingers.

I screamed and ripped off the sheet. The hole was there, pulsar pink and dripping and infinite, but no hand was sticking out of it. Maybe I'd imagined that cloaked gesture—somehow both friendly and malevolent. No way Ben was still alive in there.

"What the fuck?" Carter said, wiping the crust from his eyes and squinting at the hole. "Is that—"

"Yeah," I said, my voice shaky. "Happy birthday, I guess."

Carter rubbed his temples and let out a shuddering, bone-tired breath. The first hangover of his thirties.

"Fuck," he said. "Do you think it's safe?"

"Probably not," I said. "Why? Do you want to try it?"

I wouldn't let him, but something drove me to

ask the question anyway.

"No, no," he said. "I just …"

He looked away, his cheeks reddening.

Of course, he wanted to try the hole. Maybe he was more like Ben than I'd thought, only with a slower creep toward the single-minded pursuit of sexual novelty and extremity. I'd seen the first hint of it last night with his tofu-soft dick, nothing I did able to please him. A few more months together and he'd be done with me unless I offered him something exceptionally perverse. I held back tears.

"Hey, are you okay?" Carter asked.

His question lessened my fears a little. Ben never would have asked me that even if I'd been full-on crying.

"I need to know," I said. "Can you be happy with me even without trying the hole?"

He hesitated a moment, then nodded.

I would have felt relief had it not been for his pause. Did it contain disappointment? Deception? Or was I just paranoid after everything Ben put me through?

I decided not to push the issue.

"Alright, well, I need to drink some water," Carter said, sliding out of bed. "My head fucking hurts."

When he popped into the bathroom, I was alone. Well, not entirely. It was me and the hole. Something unseen squelched around inside, dragging itself toward some deeper recess. Maybe this thing had eavesdropped on my conversation with Carter. A little check-in from some grotesque dimension beyond the stars.

I couldn't be sure if it was Ben, but I knew—for better or worse—that he'd never truly leave me.

WRAPPED IN GOLDEN SILK

Elizabeth Lynn Blackson

"Price is no object," Mrs. Caroline Arrington said. Her eyes wandered over the woman sitting across the cafe table from her.

The woman was just known as Tigrosa, probably the hot rising star in the fashion designer scene, and Mrs. Arrington caught on early to this budding talent. She had wisely become a patron, and watched this amazing thing blossom. Now, the relationship was about to bear fruit.

"Price isn't the issue," Tigrosa said. "There are only so many craftsfolk. This isn't an industrial-scale process. There have only ever been four garments made of spider silk. Ever. And the three modern pieces took five years apiece."

"You have a year. And, as I said, price is no object. I expect results," Mrs. Arrington said. "The temperament of the Gods of fashion are fickle, and I would deeply lament having to see my patronage go to another artist. Your talent is immense, but that only matters to me if I can show it."

"Show it off, you mean," Tigrosa smiled. She leaned back in her seat. The woman seemed immune to intimidation, a trait Caroline found infinitely intriguing.

Mrs. Arrington appreciated the woman before her as the artist drew her shoulders back in a more formal posture. She reminded Caroline so much of the bust of Nefertiti, but with a more delicate chin. And below that, her breasts were full, pert, of a perfectly inviting shape, and covered by a tube of red lycra serving as a minidress. Her cleavage was a nearly irresistible lure to the eye.

She was as much art herself as her fashion.

"Of course I mean show it off," Caroline admitted. "What do you think I'm doing right now, if not putting a lovely creature on display as my lunch date."

"So, now I'm your date?" Tigrosa lifted a foot, and very lightly brushing her toe, exposed through open toed red stilettos, along Caroline's calf.

Caroline smiled, perhaps blushing a bit. "It's not nice, teasing an old woman."

Tigrosa smiled. "Who said it was a tease?" She let the statement hang in the air for a moment. "And I'd hardly call thirty-seven old. Give me a year, and I will wrap you in golden spider silk," she assured her patron.

* * *

Caroline stood in the foyer of Tigrosa's Manhattan apartment. The view was good. It wasn't Billionaire's Row, but it said a lot about what Tigrosa had achieved. She showed immaculate taste in every detail of the space.

Tigrosa's fame had grown. Her name had practically exploded into the spotlight after an enormously successful publicity stunt where she was bound to a rock, and seemingly attacked by a big, winged monster, broadcast on international news. Since then, she had shown up on the elbows of some of the biggest names amongst the billionaire elite playboys. Frequently, when the scissor doors of the exotic supercars opened, it was Tigrosa behind the wheel, not her date.

Caroline was left breathless by the wonderful audacity of it all. The…flamboyance.

As always, Tigrosa wore a dress that was nothing more than a simple tube of red lycra that hugged her from just above her areolas to just below her vulva, and sometimes, Caroline had noticed, not quite that far. It hid nothing of her long, toned legs, her full curved hips, tapering to a pleasantly slim waist. All of this with—and she hated the word, but it felt so apt—'exotic' features. The skin tone, a warm latte, was absolutely free of defects. The silky curtain of fine black hair so dark that highlights were almost blue.

Tigrosa's eyes were nearly black around the outside of the iris, fading to a shockingly bright blue. Caroline stared at those eyes with a hawk-like scrutiny. She'd seen laser procedures to remove eye pigment change even dark brown eyes to a steel gray/blue, but she had no idea there was a way to enhance the brightness of the blue pigment so dramatically. The eyes faded from twilight blue, to the color of mid-day sky. They weren't colored contacts. Caroline could spot those from a mile away. They had to be natural. There was no way to fake them.

In fact, despite Tigrosa being a flawless specimen of beauty, Caroline could not find a single unnatural enhancement. Celestial beings themselves must have ordained her beauty, it was so perfect.

All of this, and a face that could transform from regal to impish to an absolute childlike innocence in a moment.

And she had luscious lips.

Caroline felt her heart flutter, imagining those lips tenderly pressed to her labia, while Tigrosa delicately licked and gently nibbled her clitoris. She was blushing, she was sure.

Tigrosa smiled a warm greeting, The sound of her stiletto heels echoed slightly as she approached.

Tigrosa was tall, and the heels only emphasized it. Caroline had to turn her chin up slightly to meet Tigrosa's gaze.

She slipped into Caroline's space, and with a quick dart of her eyes, seemed to take in every detail. She slid her arms around Caroline's waist, giving little kiss-kisses to both cheeks, and pulled her head away.

"You look as magnificent as ever, Mrs. Arrington."

The name was a wound, a wedge of formality, an unpleasant deference. "Call me Caroline, please," she said sincerely.

That look of impishness returned, the one that made Caroline's heart race. "Caroline," Tigrosa echoed. The impishness deepened, tinged with excitement. "I have the first piece."

She wheeled and walked away. Sashayed. Was it a sashay, a signal, or just how she always moved?

Did she naturally walk with a catwalk strut? Was it just second nature from doing fashion shows? Caroline tried to reign in her wants… needs… deep, animal desires.

The woman in red picked up a matte black box, about one by two feet, and six inches deep. Inside, delicate crepe paper covered a golden garment.

Caroline opened it to find a brilliant, golden-hued brocaded overbust corset.

She lifted the impossibly light fabric. It had a texture with some of the smooth gloss of regular silk, but with a strange grabby quality, like the slightest reluctance to let go.

"That is four months of work," Tigrosa explained. "That gold color is the natural material. Golden Orb-weaver Spiders' silk. The most exotic material I can imagine. The spider theme is carried through in the brocade." She ran perfectly manicured red nails down the lustrous fabric. "Let's try it on for fit, shall we?"

Caroline stood frozen for a moment. The sudden sense of vulnerability, of being naked to any great degree in front of this beautiful woman gave her pause. She had disrobed in front of a hundred servants, shopkeepers, fashion designers, and photographers. A brief modeling career that catapulted her into the arms of one of the richest men on Earth left her with almost no body-shyness.

She had only ever felt any sense of self consciousness around her lovers.

Her need broke the mental barrier. She set her clutch on a glass table, and started taking off her jewelry.

“Once the rest is done, we can talk about accessories for the outfit,” Tigrosa said, eyes still on Caroline. “Obviously gold, but it’s important that the fabric is the main attraction. Well, the fabric and the figure in it.”

Caroline unzipped her light, silk dress and stepped out of it revealing a lovely demicup bra with front closure.

“Very nice,” Tigrosa said approvingly, with a single fingernail flick to indicate the lingerie. “You’ve always had such beautiful taste.” She paused for a moment, staring at Caroline’s cleavage.

Caroline felt like she was about to hyperventilate.

“The bra, too, love,” Tigrosa finally said, teasingly.

“Oh,” Caroline managed.

The bra fell away.

Again, Tigrosa’s eyes flicked over her, judging. A smile spread on those beautiful red lips. “Nice.” She said appreciatively. “Your figure is absolutely sumptuous.” She held the corset, and moved behind Caroline. Tigrosa wrapped the smooth, cool material around her, and Caroline felt the delicate brush of the silk across her nipples. They hardened in response. Her heart hammered in her chest and she felt the tickle of Tigrosa’s fingers near her spine, lacing the corset. She shivered.

“Are you alright? I’m not hurting you, am I?” Tigrosa asked.

“No, I’m just…” Caroline had no way to put it into words.

"Touch deprived, I'd say," Tigrosa finished gently, her chin just touching the edge of Caroline's ear.

Caroline sighed. "I suppose so," she admitted sadly.

"I hope you won't think this too forward of me," Tigrosa said, before reaching over Caroline's left shoulder, slipping manicured fingers into the left cup of the corset, and gently lifting Caroline's breast, adjusting it into the corset perfectly. Fingertips brushed her nipple, sending cold shivers down her scalp and legs.

Caroline shivered harder, and her knees felt weak.

Tigrosa's right arm wrapped around her waist, supporting her. It seemed effortless. "I have you. Am I alright to adjust the other side?"

Caroline managed a nod. Tigrosa's full breasts pressed into her near her trapezius muscles, almost rested on her shoulders, and Caroline felt herself getting aroused. She was simultaneously thrilled and slightly humiliated. It would be worse if Tigrosa saw the wet spot growing on her panties. Would that be worse?

Life as a wife of a Billionaire left her in a place of power, and she used that power, bending others to her will. But using that power was so exhausting. She longed to relent, to release those reins of control. To be the weaker. The Submissive. She wanted to be small, delicate and… weak… for Tigrosa. But most of all, she wanted Tigrosa to know that, to somehow intuit this unspeakable desire. She didn't know how to find the courage to admit she wanted to be weak.

Tigrosa reached in to adjust the right cup. The only thing holding Caroline on her feet was Tigrosa's left arm around her. Tigrosa's left hand was firmly against her belly.

"Come on," Tigrosa said curtly. "Up you go. You have to have proper posture while I lace you in."

Caroline snapped to, responding to the gentle yet authoritarian command.

Tigrosa pulled cords, cinching the corset.

Caroline wheezed out slightly. "Oh. Oh, my God."

"Are you alright?"

"Absolutely. Give me a second, then you can pull again… Okay."

Tigrosa tugged harder.

Caroline's ribcage constricted. Her waist reduced to about twenty three inches. "Okay. One more."

Tigrosa gave a strong tug. Caroline gave a little gasp, and took several tiny puffs of breath.

Tigrosa ran her hands around the tiny waist, along the hips. She slipped around to Caroline's front, and looked at her face, which had flushed pink. She stepped back to take in Caroline's figure for a moment. Caroline watched in horror, as those eyes… those eyes that could take in every detail with a glance… came to rest looking down… at the growing wet spot in her panties.

The humiliation transformed as Caroline watched Tigrosa's nipples harden through impossibly thin, tight red lycra. She watched Tigrosa's lips deepen in color, and swell invitingly.

"Oh..." Tigrosa said. It was the first time Caroline had ever heard 'coy' from her.

Tigrosa blinked and the smile turned impish. "Oh... If you're... interested..."

"Tigrosa..." She broke her chains of propriety. "Would you touch me? Please? Make me yours. Make me feel... desirable."

Tigrosa leaned in, with understanding in her eyes. She ran manicured nails into Caroline's expensive hairdo, grasped a handful of hair and pressed her lips to Caroline's. They breathed each other's air.

Tigrosa wrapped her arms around Caroline, and hugged her warmly. She moved her hands lower, cupped her ass, and squeezed.

Caroline chirped, "Ah!" in surprise, then started laughing.

"You are beautiful," Tigrosa told her. "I will wrap you in silk, and the world will desire you. Your visage will live forever."

* * *

Caroline swept up a pile of documents, and passed them to her personal assistant. Men in fashionable suits milled about the conference room. On any other day, every ounce of attention would be on driving these people like a team of coordinated oxen. Getting them to get something accomplished that made the corporation money. But the text from Tigrosa came in yesterday. The next bit of her outfit was ready and with wanton abandon, she had canceled and rescheduled meetings that left fortunes in question. They did not matter. She drifted into the elevator, across the lobby, and into a waiting limo. She could not concentrate on anything but the thought of Tigrosa wrapping her in silk.

Again, she went through the process of having the corset laced in place. It was again an exquisite, if all too brief experience. When Tigrosa finished, she reached for what looked like spools of ribbon, the same rich golden color as the corset.

"So, here's what I was thinking…" she said, attaching the ribbons at the corners of the corset's cups and others at the back, then wrapping them, one clockwise, one counterclockwise, in a crisscrossing pattern down Caroline's arms, and finishing with bows that allowed about eight inches of excess from each ribbon. The cool touch of the material and delicate touch of Tigrosa caused goosebumps to run down her arms and legs.

"I swear, if I didn't know any better, I'd think you were a rope bunny," Tigorsa laughed.

"What's a rope bunny?" Caroline asked. The moment she did, she regretted it.

Maybe.

The puckish smile returned to Tigrosa's face. She stepped away, wheeled on a heel, and gestured with one beckoning finger. Caroline followed, to the bedroom.

Within, she saw a mannequin in the shape of a woman, wearing an elaborate pattern of rope bindings. There was also a large, sturdy looking A-frame of steel tubing, large enough to stand under.

"Have you ever heard of shibari?" Tigrosa asked, moving to the mannequin. She gently rubbed her red nails over the ropes, occasionally plucking at them, like someone playing a stringed instrument.

"Jesus, that's… elaborate," Caroline said, almost breathlessly.

"Oh… I thought maybe we could do sandals for your outfit and run bindings up your legs, rather like this style. What do you think?"

Caroline could not pay attention. She couldn't get her mind past those red nails plucking at the cords. She couldn't get over imagining herself in that harness. She was sweating, thinking of the delicious powerlessness of such bondage.

"Caroline…?" Tigrosa asked, after a moment. "What do you think?"

"I think I want you to tie me up," Caroline blurted.

Tigrosa smiled, and retrieved a measure of rope. She turned, and touched a pair of emergency shears on a table. "If you say 'Red', or 'Red Light', anything like that, I stop. Alright? If you start to panic, and want out, say 'black'. Anything like that, and I'll cut you free. We stop if I get the slightest sense of your displeasure. Alright?"

Caroline nodded, breathing shallow little gasps, nearly high on endorphins.

Like the silk, it was smooth against Caroline's skin, and over minutes, the length was used to bind her knees.

"And now we weave rope in with the ribbons on your arms…" Tigrosa laced from one arm, behind

Caroline's back to the other, back and forth. "How is your range of motion? No shoulder issues?"

"No. I'm good," Caroline said.

Tigrosa pulled the lacing between the arms, and Caroline's forearms pulled together behind her back. Tigrosa pulled slowly, making sure Caroline's shoulders were all right. "You do yoga, don't you?"

Caroline laughed nervously.

Tigrosa tossed another bit of rope over the A-frame, and gently guided Caroline to stand her under the beam of the A-frame. "This spider silk is from Golden Orb Weaver Spiders. A friend of mine told me about Japanese folklore, where there is a creature called a Jorogumo, a shapeshifting spider woman that transformed into a Golden Orb Weaver."

"Is that what you are?" Caroline asked, breathlessly. "Are you a Jorogumo?"

Tigrosa laughed. "Don't be silly." She smiled impishly, while weaving the rope into Caroline's bindings. "I'm a wolf spider, not a spinner," she teased. "But I think I'm developing a real fondness for weaving webs." She pulled with her entire body weight, and Caroline felt her feet lifted from the floor.

She was suspended, comfortably cradled in golden silk, trussed up like a morsel. She could barely breathe, both from arousal and constriction.

As she hung there, Tigrosa plaited her hair, weaving golden threads into it. When finished, she pulled the threads together. She lashed them to arm bindings, forcing her head back. She ran red nails across Caroline's throat, before moving to pick up the shears.

She knelt between Caroline's legs. "I was thinking about doing some rope work down here…if you're alright with it. I don't want to unbind your legs, so I thought…" She snipped the shears in the air. "Maybe I'd just cut your panties away."

Caroline gasped and wriggled.

Tigrosa raised the shears and cautiously snipped the silky material first on one side, then the other. The tattered panties were only held in place by Caroline's thighs. Tigrosa gripped the material, and pulled up and away. The material pulled tight against Caroline's vulva, then slid between the labia as it was pulled away, gently sliding against her clitorus. Tigrosa stood, holding the remnants of the panties. She eyed them before moving them closer to her face, taking in the scent of the wet fabric. She smiled and dropped them.

She cautiously threaded more thin cord between Caroline's legs, forming a harness that pinched her vulva gently. With a delicate touch, she adjusted the repeated loops of cord into neat rows, nails brushing Caroline's labial folds, sending shocks of electricity through Caroline.

"You are absolutely a rope bunny," Tigrosa laughed.

* * *

Caroline stepped across the threshold of Tigrosa's apartment. She was wrapped in golden silk, bejeweled in gold and fine, sparkling precious gemstones. She was radiant, a vision of splendor.

She was also more than a little tipsy.

She stumbled into Tigrosa's waiting arms.

"Oopsie," she said, smiling up into those exquisite eyes.

"It looks like the soiree went well," Tigrosa said, smiling.

"It certainly went. And I was… the center of attention." She gestured grandly. "I think… What's that joke? I think my husband is about to trade in his forty for two twenties. Jesus… I thought the day might come but…" she stopped. She had to. "He barely even looks at me any more. Well, despite how my husband acted, other men seemed quite appreciative." Her tone turned sad. "I watched their eyes wander over me, in lust and admiration. Probably for the last time in my life, I turned every head in a room. And all I wanted at that moment was… you. Your eyes on me. For you to see something beautiful and desirable in me. I wanted so badly for you to want me. To make me yours, completely."

Tigrosa continued to smile, wrapped her arms around Caroline, and pulled her close. It was so forceful, it left Caroline breathless, staring up into those exotic eyes. She melted with submission.

Tigrosa led her to the bedroom, to the A-frame, to bondage.

Caroline followed, willingly.

"Tonight," Tigrosa said lovingly, "I will make you mine, completely."

Delicate fingers wove. There were no course ropes this time. Only fine lines of spider silk.

Caroline nearly fell into a trance as she was constricted and contorted, until her breath was barely the stirring of butterflies.

Tigrosa's fingers danced over her. They felt like spiders, with the immaculate red nails delicately plucking at the strings, sending almost musical vibrations through Caroline.

She came back to herself and realized she was suspended, legs folded at the knees and bound. Arms behind her and bound, head back, throat exposed. At Tigrosa's mercy.

"I'm yours," she whispered.

"I know," Tigrosa said lovingly. With one perfectly lacquered nail, she touched Caroline's chin and guided their lips together.

Tigrosa breathed in, sucking away something that was very much not air.

Caroline felt her very essence being tugged. She gasped, in a moment of fear, then relented. Instead, she tumbled into a beautiful abyss of unbeing.

"I wrapped you in golden silk," Tigrosa said. "adorned you with gold, and you still weren't satisfied. There is no lover, no toy, no accomplishment that could fill that void in you. That endless hunger for more. That tragedy, wrapped in glittering gold was simply… delicious."

Tigrosa feasted on Caroline's essence, until there was nothing left. She stared for a moment at the lifeless body, a shell of flesh, now devoid of all Essence.

They had been watching and waiting. When Tigrosa relented, thousands of orb weaver spiders skittered in from the shadowy corners of the ceiling to descend like a slow rain.

They began to feast on the body.

The life's work of thousands of spiders were woven around Caroline's remains. The spiders would eat the garments of spider silk along with the corpse, until nothing remained but gold jewelry.

Gold, and the lingering taste of Caroline's delicious tragedy.

BRIDE TO THE QUEEN OF WINTER

Marisca Pichette

Wrapped in December snow,
our legs twined like contortionists
in the bed of a white queen's sleigh.

I painted my fingertips with frostbite,
licking powder snow from her lips
& lying & laughing & lying anew.

Between us: tin fever-red, frozen open
cubes rigid & forgiving
sugar-coated lust.

She drew her sleigh beside me
& offered a treat
no witch can resist.

Toadstool delight, Turkish death
wrapped in January flurries &
sticky with desire.

We shared a bite that stung—
wind erasing my past as easily
as poison subsumes blood.

AN OFFERING OF MEAT

Amanda Nevada DeMel

January 8

I had been feeding the house scraps of raw meat for months before the crows arrived. I shoved dripping slabs into the drains, burned them in the fireplace, stowed them in the attic. Only recently have my calls been answered. I found the first one on the kitchen counter, then another under the bed. One was at the foot of the stairs, one was in the coat closet, and another was sleeping in the bathtub. By the time I found them, they were already fully grown.

I discovered the large egg shells later and had to sweep their speckled shards from the corners. They scraped on the floor with a hollow, screeching noise as I moved them. A filmy membrane connected some pieces. Although their bond seemed tenuous, it was strong enough to withstand the dragging. Just like our bond is strong enough to withstand this trial.

Now I have to be careful with the next steps. Will the neighbors be suspicious, or even aware, of the sudden influx of crows?

Obviously, I need to leave the house every so often to keep up appearances. That's how I know that the crows wait outside too. They sit on the telephone wires and watch us all, not just me. They are my protectors, ready to pluck out the eyes of anyone who dares commit a malicious act against me. I summoned them, after all. I am their benefactor.

They wake me in the morning when they need more meat. It must be fresh, or they get angry. I used dinner leftovers first. They refused to take a bite. I discreetly picked up roadkill in the middle of the night, but that was even worse to them. They huddled by the windows as if they couldn't bear the smell, as if they weren't scavengers. I tried defrosting a flank several weeks ago, just to save some money. Their caws were shrill, deafening, furious. They practically ran me out of the house and to the butcher.

Does the butcher suspect anything? He recognizes me and takes my order with a smile, but he never asks what I need with so many pounds of meat each week. How would I even answer such a question? Say that I host banquets every Saturday? Pretend that I cook for my ravenous, aging parents or the homeless? No, I can't keep track of another lie. I'd have to tell some sort of the truth.

But I don't need to worry about that now. The butcher doesn't seem even mildly interested in what I do. The fact that I pay with cash is enough for him.

The birds are getting restless, chirping and creeping closer to my studio. I must sign off this letter now, my love. It's time for dinner.

* * *

The first day Philippa had to leave the birds was a Monday. A few had hatched that weekend, squawking and begging for a task. She told them that six crows were not enough, that she had to summon more. It was a tricky situation. She had to place meat around the house and make sure that the crows who had already arrived didn't eat it all. It pained her to round them up and lock them in the attic. Force didn't work. Their intelligence warned them that she was up to something. She had to bribe them with fresh blood, then quickly close the door. Their irate caws followed her to work.

Finally in the office, safe inside its walls, she tuned out their laments. She showed her boss, Harold, her latest illustration, one of a voluptuous woman in a new brassiere and stockings. The image was perfectly striking, cutting off right above the full lips, leaving the identity of the woman a mystery. But Harold didn't find it quite right for the advertisement.

"It's just too risque," he said. "She doesn't look like your typical housewife."

She wondered how she could create an advertisement for lingerie without a risque factor. Harold sent her home with her portfolio and said he would call when another opportunity came in. It was a terse promise, accepted without much faith.

As she packed up the display, a bang startled her. It came from the window, where a thin smear of bright red blood now colored the glass. Her chest tightened, but from excitement or anxiety, she could not tell. Looking down three stories to the sidewalk, she saw a black mass fluttering in the gentle breeze. Feathers glittered in the midday light.

Her eyes bulged.

She gasped.

She had left them alone too long, and now

they had come searching for her. Or could more crows be answering her calls? Setting her hat on her head, she rushed out of the conference room and down the stairs.

When she emerged from the building, a strong wind stole her breath, freezing her in place just outside the doors. She stood over the dead bird and took in the gristle and gore. With tears streaming down her cheeks, she murmured apologies and avoided the gaze of onlookers. She looked like a well-dressed madwoman.

* * *

March 25

I'd love to paint the birds mid-meal. Imagine one crow throwing a chunk of muscle into the air, waiting for it to fall into his open beak. Two birds crouch behind him, ripping a rack of ribs to shreds. Their beaks will be stained maroon and their feet will dance on the carcasses of the weak.

My heart beats faster at the thought of laying the image onto canvas for the next generations, capturing the viscera with my brush.

But my paintings develop with an aching sluggishness, and I have no money for a camera. If I were to paint based on photographs, the result would be a cheap, lifeless mimicry anyway. Perhaps the feast is too sacred to be properly captured. My mind's eye must suffice. I hope my written descriptions will be adequate for you, my love, since you cannot be here.

Soon, though, the crows will find you. They are incredibly smart creatures, you know. They've already brought me one of your hair clips that I lost. I hold the small trinket close to me, and I sleep with it under my pillow.

When I am gone, you will still have their company for some time. I know you'll respect my wishes for a cremation, even though it will be hard for you to know that I could never return. The birds who brought you back to me will give you comfort. It's not that I don't want to come back for you after my death. It is, in fact, a selfless matter. As my body burns, the crows too will turn to ash. You see, they are demanding. They need their meat, a clean place to nest, constant company. You deserve an easy life after I go. I couldn't leave you with the burden of their care.

Oh, my Johanna, let's not think about those impending dark days. Instead, let's anticipate our reunion.

I can see us, even now, sitting in the park and feeding the pigeons like we used to do. Remember how greedy they were, how they all tried to push each other away for one more bread crumb? Do you remember how feisty the injured ones were? The ones missing toes and feet were even more aggressive than their fully-bodied counterparts. Yet we loved each one. I haven't gone to the park since I've been alone. There is simply too much to do in preparation for your return.

The crows are causing quite a stench upstairs. I laid down newspapers to cover the floor, and I add more daily. Rummaging through trash cans for discarded papers is far from pleasant, and it hurts my back, but knowing that the birds will one day find you makes the pain worthwhile. Can you imagine the impression our home would make on the neighbors if they ever dropped by? They'd smell the bitter feces, hear the sharp caws and dull thumps, and leave running. I appreciate the distance we give each other, the neighbors and I. It makes the work so much easier. It makes my stockpile of lies easier to keep track of too.

By the time you read this, we'll already have been reunited, of course, so I suppose I'll have to look forward to your homecoming on my own, while you do the same wherever you are. Perhaps we'll read these notes together and laugh at my foolish worries. The birds will laugh too.

* * *

The crows soon outgrew the attic. Philippa's heart ached when she saw how cramped the room was becoming. The birds deserved comfort and ample space. She could tell that they were unhappy, hearing their cries from downstairs. They were even throwing themselves at the door, sending dull thuds resounding through the house.

She cleared out the guest room on the second floor and left the furniture in the hallway. Then she shoved some cuts of pork, slippery and slimy and dark pink, into the far corners, grimacing as the fluids stained the white walls. Separating only a portion of the birds would be difficult, she knew, but their conditions were so inhumane right now. How many crows were crammed into the tight, stuffy attic? She had lost count. Nonetheless, it was her responsibility to ensure their wellbeing.

A crow flung itself at the attic door as Philippa walked up the stairs. They smelled their food and grew restless. Philippa noticed that some of them were injured, small gashes glistening with drying blood on their sides. They must have been starving and turned on each other to survive. And it was her fault. She thanked whoever was looking out for her that none had died.

Philippa inhaled deeply to steady herself, ignoring the biting odors of feces and dirty feathers. She ran through her plan once more and opened the door. One bird took flight as several others hopped toward her. They would not wait. She threw the slab of meat into the room, distracting many of the birds, and retreated to the guest room. With another chunk of beef hanging from her rear pocket, she lured several crows out of the attic. She walked into the guest room and stopped for a moment to listen to the clamor. The squawks of hunger, the ripping of tendons, the clack of talons, the beating of wings. She was suspended in time for a moment, lost in the symphony of her making. Before she could turn around, a crow pecked at her backside, tearing her jeans to get to the meat. There was a wet plop as the juicy cut fell to the floor.

Philippa dashed out of the room, a sharp pain on her left side hindering her speed. She slammed the attic door shut. Only two crows escaped to the hallway, but she was able to herd them back into the guest room, which soon housed at least a dozen birds, several of which were fighting over the meat. They had already found all the stashes. Black feathers rested on the bay window. Blood stained the floorboards.

One bird didn't seem interested in the sacrifice. Its light blue eyes pierced Philippa as she shut the door.

* * *

August 13

I've taken to praying at night. It's not the kind of prayer that I recited to summon the crows. It's a more traditional one, a more accepted prayer. Of course I trust the birds to find you, but I pray that I will survive long enough for our reunion. The habit isn't something I'm proud of. It feels like a surrender, to call upon a single, supposedly omniscient entity to help sort my worries and problems. It feels like a lie. Even so, praying gives me some hope, some strength. These days, I need all the strength I can get.

I won't lie. I'm afraid of them. I look on them with reverence and love, but a sense of danger hides in the corners. If I don't satisfy their every need, I know I will suffer. I want to satisfy them, I need to satisfy them. But a niggling question whispers, "Is this just self-preservation?"

* * *

She walked into the butcher's, dodging eye contact with anyone and everyone, as usual, and waited in line. When she got up to the counter, she asked for seven pounds of beef brisket. It was sold out.

"Sorry, darling," the butcher said. "We got some real tender strip steak and porter house. No? Wouldn't work? Well then, how about you forget about cooking for a night, and you and me go out?"

The blood rushed to her face. She struggled to find words, looking anywhere but the butcher's face for an answer. The eyes of the customers behind her drilled into her back.

"My parents," she finally said. "I can't leave them home alone for too long."

The butcher narrowed his eyes, and then his face broke out in a smile.

"Maybe next time, eh?" he said with a wink. "When you come in Wednesday, ask for Howie."

He had taken note of her, and he knew her schedule. She wondered if she should try a different butcher's shop not just today, but in the future too. She had to shake him off.

"Will do," Philippa lied. "Thanks, How—"

A woman's shriek interrupted her goodbye. They turned to the door, where a crow had affixed itself to someone's hair. Its wings beat with grand, laborious movement, as if it were trying to heft the weight and fly away with it. All the while, the woman's eyes, round as the crow's, darted from person to person, pleading for help. She thrashed her arms, beat her head, and screamed, yet no one moved to help her.

The other patrons backed farther into the store, watching the scene unfold with equal horror and fascination. They looked like they were in a cinema, so invested in a film.

"Jesus Christ," Howie mumbled. "Not again."

Only then did fear set in. The birds knew where she got their meals, evidently. What else did they know? How often had they stormed the shop in disbelief that Philippa would provide for them? Maybe that was why they hadn't yet found their target: their demands had not been satisfied.

Howie grabbed a mop from behind the counter and charged at the woman. She was still screaming, still waving her arms in an attempt to dislodge the crow, but now she backed toward the door.

"Stand still, lady," the butcher said.

He lifted the mop and shoved the handle at the bird. Philippa felt a pain in her own chest as the crow was jabbed. He thrust the handle once, twice, three, four times before the crow flew off. She was winded, the air knocked out of her lungs. As Howie apologized to the crying woman for the scare, Philippa ran back home. She needed to make sure that the rest of them were okay and, more importantly, that they were contained.

* * *

September 29

Where are you, my darling? Nearly eleven months have I spent alone with the crows. I don't doubt their skills. They bring me small gifts, little items to remind me of you. A comb, a barrette with a purple rhinestone, a nearly-empty tube of lipstick. I do love them, our little saviors, but I want <u>you</u>.

The butcher — whose name is evidently Howie — eyes me lasciviously every time I walk in. The fool thinks I frequent his shop to see him. Sure, I smile back, but only to be kind. If he weren't the only butcher in walking distance, I wouldn't return. Still, the meat is so heavy and the walk is so long to begin with.

Don't worry, my love. A coy smirk is all he will ever get. I save myself for you, Johanna. One day we will reunite, our love will rekindle, our life will continue. But when?

It's been roughly five weeks since I've had to buy more paint. I'm at a terrible standstill. My hand refuses to hold a brush.

Harold hasn't called me since April. I hate to say it, but I'm now living on our savings. What's the use of art if none of it sells? I'm sure you'd have something wise to say in response, something about the value of the self, but none of that seems factual without you.

Sometimes I feel as if the birds are close to finding you. I can't say why I feel that, though. It's a sensation in both my chest and my head, a tightness and a lightness. I close my eyes and see you walking home. You still have that charming limp, so I rush to help you. When you see me, you start crying, smiling, apologizing. Of course, there's no need for you to ever feel sorry. That's what love is: forgiveness. Any strife you may have caused is already forgiven.

The time is half past five. The birds have been getting hungry earlier. Their squawks are shriller, their behavior more aggressive. When I bring the huge slabs of dripping, tender meat, they very nearly ambush me. They pull and rip anything they can get their beaks on. I've taken to wearing gardening gloves when I go upstairs.

Their odor is everywhere. Your pillow no longer smells of your perfume and cold cream.

* * *

She opens the attic door, a light sheen of sweat on her body. The only exposed skin is on her face, and they spot that before they notice the huge rack of ribs she holds. A yelp escapes her lips as one flies at her head. She drops the meat, which distracts a few of them, but most are fixated on her body. They stare at her with visible disdain and triumph. The crow that flew at Philippa circles, then lands on her hair. The slow pull of gravity brings its solid feces down through the strands. She doesn't care about that right now.

"Johanna?"

She stares at the woman sitting on the windowsill. Her blond hair is beautifully coiffed, without a single flyaway.

Philippa takes a step forward and slips on a clump of feathers connected to a black wing only by a string of gristle. She lands on the hard floor, and the curve of a rib juts into her back. Her tailbone shrieks in pain and her clothing absorbs the dampness from the waste, but still she doesn't care. The layers of newspaper covering the floor slide on each other, excrement acting as concrete that hasn't yet solidified. The papers squelch as Philippa settles.

Let my body cover with bruises, let my shirt soil, she thinks.

Only one thing holds her attention.

"Johanna?"

Something sharp jabs at her midriff. She tears her gaze away from her love to find a crow, beak bloodied, perched on her hip. Her shirt had ridden up and exposed a patch of flesh when she fell. There is a small crevice, just left of her navel, pooling with blood. She looks up and sees that Johanna remains seated on the windowsill. She has a faraway look in her eyes, though her gaze is settled on her old lover.

Philippa reaches out to her, but the pressure from bending her stomach is too much to bear. It feels like a torrent of liquid seeps out from the hole. More birds have come to rest on her. Two peck at her torso. One weighs down her shoulder. She tries to shake them off, but any flexing of her abdomen causes more blood to spurt and black stars to shoot in her vision.

"Johanna," she murmurs as she lets her head fall on the floor.

She's come back to me.

Her flesh is set ablaze with each incision as another crow breaks her skin. Rivulets of blood stream down her sides and collect in her clothing. As the birds pull at her muscle, she feels the stretch of her body, then the ripping and separation.

This is all for Johanna. The current pain may be excruciating, but it pales in comparison to the emotional turmoil she experienced when Johanna left. It may not be as she intended, but Philippa knows they will be together again, somehow, somewhere. The birds have served their purpose.

UNTETHERED WORLD

Ezra Wu

As this life furls tighter around me, I remember once there had been a boy, dreaming in my mind.

* * *

"These ones are yours." Fin shoved a tangle of cloth and cables into my hands.

I pried and pulled them apart, eventually untangling a pair of goggles from their wrappings. He was already wearing his, so I pulled them over my face.

"What's with these? I can't see anything through them."

"That's the point, dumbass."

The view through the goggles was reduced to a thin horizontal slit, so narrow that I could only just piece together the fragments of the world around me. The green hillside, the dusk sky, the shadowed forest were all barely decipherable. Fin, too, was only a sliver of color in a field of black.

He set off down the hill, seemingly unbothered by the goggles. I stumbled after him.

Fin arrived at the bottom of the hill long before I did. Though I was beginning to adjust, the darkness of the trees and their long shadows sent me spinning. I resisted the urge to grope around me.

Fin took pity and pulled me over by the sleeve. He had a flashlight, blinding me with it before pushing it into my hands and spinning me away from him.

"Since you're new at this I'll explain how it works. You can't look at anything. In this place, things change. They change if you look at them. They'll change if you think about them. Not only that, you'll change too."

"That doesn't make any sense. How am I supposed to not look or think about anything?"

"Well, you can't," Fin said, his voice laughing. "You can only hope it doesn't change too much."

Fin's steps crunched on the dead leaves as he took his first steps into the forest. "That said, you must absolutely not look anything in the eyes. And that includes me."

And with that, Fin stepped into the shadows of the forest, and, in my eyes, disappeared completely into the night.

The air was cool and, troubled by the occasional wind, carried its own darkness. Dusk was only minutes away, bringing with it the howl of strange creatures which I had never heard before.

I turned up the hilltop to see one last glance of the setting sun, but it was gone. Instead, there was a silhouette. Before I could stop myself, I looked into its eyes. Despite the distance, despite the gloom, I saw them clearly: Pinpricks of light, too small for the expanse of darkness of its face.

I looked away hurriedly, shone my flashlight

into the night for signs of Fin. If he was here, I could not see him. But it did not matter--I ran into the forest where I had seen him last. I did not dare look back.

* * *

I fumbled through the trees, vision alternating between slits of trunks, branches, darkness. Something caught me, pulling at my sleeve.

"Where are you going, Jack?"

My heart stopped for a moment, but I recognized the voice.

"Where are we, Fin?"

"We're in the heart of the forest, Jimmy, where we were always headed. But be careful, John, of questions like that."

That's right, I remembered, to think lightly, flittingly, stopping at no name or subject for very long.

By now the trunks had grown huge and towering. Their roots swelled to great sizes, some bulging even taller than us from the leaf-carpeted ground. All sounds were muffled, but ever present. The light of dusk made it no further than the highest branches. Beneath, with us, was darkness impenetrable.

"Fin, earlier—I know you said—I..." I could not bear to face him.

He shushed me. "Come on, we're almost there," already disappearing again.

I chased after Fin's silhouette, flickering in and out of view. Soon I lost track of it, and instead, I watched the yellowing circle of his flashlight as it flitted around from branch to trunk to leaves to ground. It never stopped anywhere for long, always gone just as the bark started to warp, the leaves started to whisper, the roots started to groan, leaving thoughts and fears to linger in the imagination and the darkness.

I wanted to ask Fin desperately what it was we were looking for, why it was that we were here, but he had cautioned against such questions, so I did my best to push them from my mind.

The circle of light stopped suddenly, coming to rest in the hollow of a tree much larger than any I had seen ever before. Its uneven illumination wavered as it traced out the entrance of the tree hollow, huge enough to fit a house. The light plunged in. I followed.

The inside of the tree was even larger. Its size could not be seen, only heard through the unending echoes of the small sounds we made with our footsteps and our breathing. It smelled of old wood, old dirt, old damp. Where his flashlight fell the wood was a deep, rich red, riddled with evergreen moss.

The tree creaked and moaned with our small attentions. I imagined the texture of its bark running into little rivers, its roots twisting and coiling into snail shells. But the tree itself was mighty, and no force could move it. I had flicked my flashlight off some time ago, and now turned it on again.

The small sounds of the tree drifted upward. I followed them with my flashlight up, into the peak of that hollow.

Through the sliver of my goggles, I saw a line of golden thread nestled up there in the hollow's highest eaves. Its distance, and therefore its size, was impossible to determine. Was it a ray of light, I wondered? A worm? A fungus?

It began to grow, thicker, brighter, closer, twisting in irregular patterns. It split, many headed, like a hydra. I saw scales and ripples, honeycomb patterns in its glowing skin. The hollow undulated with its light. It was so close now, close enough to reach...

Something knocked the breath from my lungs. I was forced off my feet and dragged from the tree. I began to struggle and was thrown onto the ground.

"Christ, Jake, what did I say?"

"Fin, I thought you were here with me."

"I lost track of you two hours ago. And then I come to find you and—"

A great rumble cut Fin off, increasing in pitch until it became a warbling hum in our ears. I looked over in the direction of the tree. Golden tendrils came crawling from its hollow in a great tangle, spreading hungrily through the grass and the branches and the air. It threw hard beams of light through the dark of the forest, which in turn solidified, warped, and began to multiply.

Their searching, questing growth halted. Then they sped toward us.

I grabbed Fin's arm.

"We have to go."

We ran in my best estimation of the way we had come. We stumbled through tree roots, clambered over and under low hanging branches. The low warbling followed at every step, but I could not spare a moment to stop and turn around. At any moment, those golden threads might reach out and ensnare us to watch them forever...

Until suddenly, we were free. We had broken clear of the forest. There was only silence amid the other small sounds of this place's night. Only the sky, pitch black and starless, and the ground beneath it. I heaved a sigh of relief.

Set against the night sky, the great tree rose over the skyline of the forest. The tranquility of the scene was in sharp contrast to our drumming hearts and staggered breath.

"That was crazy," said Fin, panting next to me. He lifted his goggles up to wipe the sweat from his brow.

"Do you think it was some sort of trap?" I asked, after I caught my breath. I looked out into the horizon, where the forest bled out into the dark sky. "Something that feeds on the change that we make?"

"No, Jason. I think that's just the way things are."

Out of the corner of my eye, I saw Fin stoop to pick something up. Something sunk into the pit of my stomach.

I turned to stop him, already calling out. In my mind's eye I saw that shadow silhouette, with eyes of small light.

But there was no one there. Fin was gone. At the ground where he stood were his goggles, and a small, smooth stone.

I looked off into the distance, across the hillside, over the forest. But there was no one around. The only movement was the wind, tousling the long grass and the uppermost of branches. Fin couldn't have left for the forest; I would have seen him go.

All that was left were his goggles and the stone. I remembered Fin taking off the goggles, but surely it was only for a moment.

My attention fell to the stone. It was round and smooth, shaped almost like an egg. Was this what Fin had been trying to pick up? Had he looked at it without his goggles? Had this small stone subsumed him?

I grabbed the stone and held it to my chest. The night seemed long and endless, the world huge and featureless, a vast expanse with no place I wanted to go.

I looked over to the great tree, the only constant in this ever-changing world. Suddenly, the wind picked up around me. It crescendoed into a great howling as it blew through the forest. The silhouette of the tree was shapeless against the night sky, and in its midst, I saw two small lights, like gleaming eyes.

The tree warped, deformed. The lights grew brighter, then began to drip trails of gold light. It spread wildly across the tree's shadow, revealing shoulders, arms, fingers. The giant lifted itself above the treeline, advancing.

I ran up the hill. Behind me, the giant tore through the forest; trees falling, footsteps thundering. The ground began to shake and tremble. As I crested the top of the hill, I stumbled and fell.

The giant was no longer just a giant, but a huge weight upon the earth, swallowing trees and the hill, churning on its own chaos, sucking in the wind and the sky into its tangle of darkness and golden thread. Each image swirled, bleeding into the next.

Black and gold mixed thread and stone and crumbled and hatched the dark silhouette with the small eyes that was Fin, face serene as if asleep while simultaneously leering, laughing. All the while, it approached, consuming the landscape into its huge, twisting maw.

It was nearly upon me now. Roots that were worms that were fingers crashed into the earth beside me while I fought to scramble away. But the strength of my legs was gone. I wanted desperately to go home, but could think of no place that would fit that description, no place that would not be swallowed by the frothing of this world.

There is nowhere to run.

I pull the goggles off my face.

* * *

"Marie? Marie, is that you? Where have you been?"

Daylight blinds my eyes. I am in front of a suburban home. Two stories, low fence, a sprawling orange tree. Immediately I know it as home. And the man calling my name is my husband.

But how did I get here? The story of my life is laid out, available to me, but I cannot find my place in it.

I open my hand, but there is nothing there, only a memory of smoothness.

And as Matthew throws his arms around me, desperately asking where I was, I wonder, what happened to that child? The stone, the shadow, the lights, Fin, where did they all go? Was it all a dream? But there was no sleep. One moment, I was a boy lost in a forbidding world, and the next, a woman at home, in her own life.

Matthew takes me inside the house. His concern fades as I settle into our daily routine. But my answers are automatic, my actions mimed.

The unreality of that dream, that ever changing world, pollutes my own. My home, my husband, my life, are so concrete and real around me. Yet, in the corner of my eye, it seems it must be changing, slowly, secretly, where I cannot see. And I, too, change with it, and do not notice its lies. I am Marie, and have been my whole life, but at the same time I am that child, still lost in that untethered world.

PIG'S BLOOD / for a pig

Anastasia Jill

They bullied me, a girl:
I know I'm gonna die,
So I'll pray,
One last time,

/ i will pray.

Hail mama, full of grace,
Mama, don't you love me?
The other girls, they laugh at me.
They know,
They know

/ i am not like them

Oh, kind-hearted teacher,
Do you see the Lord in me?
The other girls,
They pull me apart like wings from a butterfly
They laugh at me, in my cage,
Waxen rich, a cage of birds without functional wings.

They made me queen,

/ queen of not girl

/ not she

/ not her

/ let us pray

I burn the bush of God,
Wood and brimstone, bone from floor
Of the high school gym
Where I am the queen
Who longs to shed her crown

And separate them from their spines,
A fascicle made from, an anthology of hate
And a bottom full of boys;
The nice boys, the blood boys, the boys that come
And keep tally of girls like them
And as they die, I think, "Eve was weak,"

The raven of sin
Oh, but oh,
I don't have wings, I cannot fly.

but I can scream from nose and mouth,
I am not black or red,
I am pink as a teacup pig.
What color is a pig's blood?
Red, raging red, oh red.
"I might've known it might be red."

The pig, the pig is me.
Cut the pig from the soft folds

Of girl
Eve was weak;

A Woman.

I am neither weak
nor a woman.
Mama—see?
I was never a woman

Buried beneath a cross
Dirt and gravel, like a skillet cooking me
Red
Bathing me
Red
Tethering me to the ground
Red and descended;

/ one day

/ i will spread

/ my girl lips

/ into fallen angel wings

A HOME IS ONLY AS WARM AS THE FLESH THAT RESIDES THERE

Minh-Anh Vo Dinh

A home is only as warm as the flesh that resides there. I can barely remember what this house used to look like. When we first moved in, it was barren, lifeless, and devoid of touch. It was simply a structure existing through time without purpose. But we made it home, you and I. We turned it into our sanctuary, where all the noise and chaos could never reach us. In our home, only we existed and nothing else. Time moved quickly and slowly all the same in this house as we watched it course by us like a stream flowing from a river. In the coldest winters, you provided me with the warmth of your flesh and the beating of your heart. And right now, this home is cold and unforgiving.

I sometimes hear you at night. I hear you within the walls, through the pipes, and all over this house. Yet I never see you. You hate me. You hate me and you want me to know it. You think I didn't know it was you who broke those glasses so I would step on them? Or was it not you who slammed the doors and windows all night to deprive me of sleep and sanity? And was it not you who filled the tub with visions of blood and death to frighten me? I deserve your torment, that I know. You want to punish me and break me into little pieces. Demolish my mind, my body, my soul, do it over and over until we meet again.

I want to see you. I miss you.

The world is eternal darkness, and you're the sun. You radiate warmth even if the lights have dimmed from your eyes forever. I'm sorry for taking the lights away from you. I'm sorry for burying you in the dark.

I still vividly remember the day I found you hanging from the ceiling. It was a hot summer day and the air was damp like a sauna. The windows were shut and the AC was not on. I didn't know how long you'd been up there. It smelled like days had passed.

A home is only as warm as the flesh that rots there. I sobbed while cradling your body in our bed, the bed that we had made love on many times, the bed that we had spent countless Sundays on because the mere thought of doing anything else was too much, the bed that I lay on, watching you long after you had drifted off to sleep.

Remnants of you still remain on our bed.

To scrub off your remnants is to scrub off the memories that we share, to betray the secrets that we swore would never leave the sheets, to erase your very existence. Remnants of you have become parts of this house. I have built a new sanctuary from your flesh and bones. You're mine to keep, the little pieces of you are now the foundation of our home.

You never wrote a note. I flipped the house looking for one. You were always one with a fondness for games. You liked to tease and confuse me, please and withhold from me. I never knew what you had in mind next. Even in death, I thought you would do the same, to leave a fucked up trail of breadcrumbs for me to find. But you didn't. Was this another kind of mind game?

Why did you do it? I thought we were happy. I know I wasn't always the best partner, but in the end we always pushed it through. You weren't the most open man, but I suppose it came with being a man, keeping it inside, tucking it deep into a corner that no one could access. I wish you'd let me in. I could've helped you. And now I'm going to spend every waking moment wondering what I'd done wrong for you to leave me. You faulted me for many things while we were together. Did you fault me for this, too?

A home is only as tender as the flesh that embraces me. Even when you get angry, you are gentle with me. There were times I flinched at the slightest move you made, fearing how rough you would get. You told me you were passionate. Is it passion if it only ever comes with hurt? I questioned why you equated passion with pain, and you told me queer men loved differently. This was the only time you let me into your mind. We're born into a world that wants to hurt us, so we seek tenderness through hurt, it's one and the same. Maybe that's why we're drawn to each other: a destroyer of things and an absorber of destruction.

People say death is liberation. But you are confined to this place, to me. A few nights after I decorated our home with your pieces, you came to visit. There was a tightness in the air, the same tightness that I felt in my stomach when you were around, and at that moment, I knew it was you. You make yourself known with the slamming of the door, in life and death. Are you angry in death, too? Are you angry that you can't leave this place? Even when you're cruel, I want to comfort you.

Why haven't you shown yourself? It's been months. I wonder if you're enjoying making me wait. It's part of who you are, to drain me until I'm hollowed out, forced to crawl at your feet and beg for a sip of your attention and care. I should hate you for tormenting me, but I don't. Because in a way, I enjoy working for your attention, for just a glance, a graze, anything at all. Only you could push me to the edge of sanity and somehow reel me back at the very last second. You would rather torment me with your ghostly tricks, like a child who has discovered a new game. I wish I could cuss you out and leave this place, but I won't. I once considered burning this place to the ground, but I can't.

The cold winter air passes through the house, and I can feel its emptiness for the first time. The cruel howling of the wind assaults me, and I wonder if your voice travels with it, laughing at me for still holding on. You've stopped playing with me as well. I would walk around the house waiting for the lights to flicker, for the window to blow open, but nothing. I bet you're just in the corner watching with that devious smile, knowing that you've won. Yes, you've won. My darling man, I will always let you win.

The lights have gone out. Sitting in the darkness in the midst of the desolate wintry night, I feel closer to you. Is this what it's like for you? Eternally in a state of limbo, chilled to the bone in a void of blackness. If you're still here, please embrace me just once, I crave your touch.

No matter what happens, I will be here. I'm in our nest, on our bed, my nose in the sheets, blackened and stained from your decay. I wish it was actually you. This is all I have left of your physical existence. In the briefest of seconds, I want to call my mother. She's expecting me for Christmas. She'll be waiting for me as I will be for you.

The harsh winter can engulf me, and I will wait for you. The sanctuary that I rebuilt from your flesh and bones can collapse on me, and I will wait for you. You may never show your face, perhaps not because you don't want to, but because you can't. Your tricks and games are not ways of torment, but ways of affection. Tenderness, hurt, pleasure, pain, I welcome it all. No matter what it is, I know for a fact you're here. And I will wait for you.

My darling man, who would I be without you? I don't exist without you, you've made sure of that. I'm just an extension of you, like a symbiosis. You will never admit it, but I know you can't exist without me either. We live and rot together, flesh and bones, time and space. Time does not exist as long as we do. And so does our home, a home so warm, so tender, so immovable as the flesh and bones that reside within its very foundation.

LOVE, LUCY
The Secret (Sapphic) Diary of Lucy Westenra
Jamie Zaccaria

5 May

This is to be my secret diary- hidden from everyone as sure as I hide my darkest secrets within its pages. I have taken to keeping another one on my nightstand lest anyone be suspicious. Should they come upon it, they will see entries of my boring daily life and could hardly imagine I had another, secret, diary hidden away.

The reason for the utmost security is that I must express my heart's aching desires and pain and can do so only within these pages. There is no one I can tell my truth to, not even dear Mina, my best friend and companion for so long. The reason I can not tell anyone, even (and especially) Mina, is because it is she who my thoughts revolve around.

I am madly, deeply, wildly in love with my dearest Mina Murray. This is more than just love for a best friend – I dream of kissing Mina, and caressing her the way I should imagine doing to a man. I can not tell another soul this and I dare not speak it to Mina herself for fear of her rejection – that is something I simply can not live with. I can not live without my dear Mina so to keep her I will quiet my lust for her.

Oh, if only Mina turned her dark eyes to me instead of that dreadfully boring Jonathan Harker. He is away to Eastern Europe and although I know it is sinful of me to say so, part of me wishes some calamity would befall him and he would never return home to steal my Mina away from me.

10 May

I've written to Mina and chided her for calling me a poor correspondent in her last letter when indeed I have written her two letters to her every one! I savor every word from my beloved although I am sick to death of hearing of Jonathan Harker. I can not fathom her feelings for the man, especially when my heart is so clearly hers. But, as the situation is, I must steady myself to live with it. I worry sometimes that someone will discover my secret.

I recently became acquainted with a Dr. John Seward who runs the lunatic asylum. I can't help but worry he will see underneath my composure and call me crazy for my love for her, maybe even commit me to be one of his patients! He is so difficult to read, with an imperturbable face, and it frightens me. In order to not be discovered I have decided that I must keep him close at hand. Oh how easy to turn a man's eye away from the truth with naught but a smile and a glance. I flirt with him to protect myself, and you, my dear Mina.

24 May

Alas, my dreams of Jonathan disappearing in Transylvania were in vain; Mina writes that he will be returning within a week. She is so in love with that boring man, it kills me. I can not spend my days of youth pining away for her, my love that I can never have. Not if I plan to make a good marriage and set my mother up for a comfortable future. I suppose it's time for me to finally make a choice. I suppose I have put off marrying someone for so long that fate has acted in jest, sending me three marriage proposals at once!

Arthur Holmwood is the only son of a lord; he is handsome, kind, and head over heels for me. Quincy is a laugh but far too adventurous for my taste and I certainly don't want to be whisked away to America and so far from Mina. I feel especially awful for flirting with Dr. Seward so hard that he seems to have fallen in love with me and thrown his hat into the ring. No, my choice must be Arthur.

If I must settle down as an old woman let it be at the same time as my dear Mina, so we may enjoy domesticity alongside one another and never part.

23 June

I have come to accept that I can not escape the fate of Mina marrying that insufferable Jonathan Harker. He and I never did quite get on, so I've been encouraging Mina in my letters to remind him or my multiple suitors and epic love story with Arthur. I must be sure he does not suspect my love for his betrothed and use it to try and keep us apart.

As for my own fiancé, I do not love Arthur but he is kind, and good, and wealthy, and dare I say even handsome. He is a fine man and will make a fine husband. Perhaps I can make myself love him?

24 July

I met Mina at the Whitby station and together we drove up to the house at the Crescent. It pains me to look at her – sweet, beautiful Mina – knowing she has my heart and I do not have hers. I wish we could stay here forever, just the two of us walking along the Esk River and admiring the green valley. I long to lay my forehead against hers, to kiss her sweet lips, and to hold her against me. I do not care if it's sinful, this is how I feel.

26 July

I have been walking in my sleep again. Mina and Mother have conspired to keep me in my chambers by locking me in at night. Every night I toss and turn, dreaming of heat and sweat between Mina and myself. I wake halfway through my shame but unable to stop staring at the source of my love and my desire.

All anyone wants to talk about is my upcoming marriage to Arthur and although it makes me anxious, I must indulge them. I'd rather have Mina by my side helping me choose new dresses and decor than anywhere out of my sight. Yet each day I feel more and more disturbed.

1 August

Mina and I had a delightful conversation with some eccentric old men who told us about the Abbey's mismatched tombstones and murdered pirates. They were quite wonderful to entertain us. As I held her hand there I realized that our time together was soon to come to an end.

6 August

The sky is gray and it feels as if electricity runs through the air. I am so jumpy; I can't help but feel something is coming, though I know not what. I relish this time with Mina but am more anxious than ever knowing they will not last. To have my heart's desire so near me and knowing her warmth will be pulled away – by Jonathan of all people. Yet, he has not been writing so perhaps he has disappeared after all. One can only hope.

8 August

A terrible storm last night! It brought more of that feeling of impending doom. Mina tells me I awakened twice in the night and got dressed, but I remember neither of these instances. I am tired and weak. I can not seem to feel awake and know my dreams have been haunted, even if I do not remember them fully.

10 August

Nothing but sadness and angst today. Attended the funeral of the poor old sea captain with dear Mina. Oh how I hate funerals, I can not bear the sadness that seeps from them. Then we heard the dreadful news that Mr. Sales had died right in the place we had sat for the funeral of some unknown shock!

Then the worst of it, somehow, was the dog. It would not stop barking and howling. I do love those creatures but felt uncertain, as if I could not ever approach it. Its owner threw it rather roughly and I almost made to step in but some fear stopped me.

Sweet Mina noticed my odd spirits and took me for a lovely walk by the cliffs to Robin Hood's Bay where we enjoyed tea in a little old-fashioned inn. If only I could freeze time and stay in that moment forever with her.

11 August

Last night was too queer. I dreamed of Mina coming to me in the dark, wearing only her thin nightgown but no shame in it. I took her hand and followed her out the door and into the night. She led me to the Abbey's churchyard and kissed me with so much passion I thought my heart would burst. There we sat under the bright moon and displayed our mutual love in ways that I dare not even put to paper for they make me blush.

I awoke terribly cold and with the awful realization that my dream was not reality. Dear Mina had found me outside in the night; I had been sleepwalking again. I can not express my crushing disappointment at being so close to my love and yet knowing it was all a fantasy of my sleep. It had felt so real that when I woke I could still sense her lips upon my face and my neck.

Before I fell back asleep (this time in my bed) I made Mina promise not to tell a soul about the incident. I don't know what is happening to me but I can not let it worry Mother.

14 August

My days have been filled with contradictions; snuggles with Mina and nightmares of giant flapping bats. I can not shake this ill feeling. Besides Mina's arms, I find much comfort in our spot on the East Cliff. The sun's rays do much to invigorate me and help me forget the strange images of my dreams. I am haunted by red eyes and blood. Are these torments punishment for my sinful love for her?

18 August

The days have been slightly better although my strange dreams persist. I am still weak and pale but being so near my love replenishes me, bringing color to my cheeks. I can bear these horrid nights of confusion and terror only because I know Mina is by my side. I must also present a happy front for Mother, who is unwell, though she tries to hide it from me.

21 August

Cursed day; Mina has left me to go back to Jonathan after receiving a letter from a hospital in Budapest where some nuns have been caring for him while he has been ill. Once again, he has torn her from my side and I feel hollow.

24 August

I have hardly any energy to write and my thoughts are consumed with missing Mina.

25 August

Without Mina's brightness, I can do nothing but wallow in my misery. Each night the dreams become more realistic and fearful, the red eyes and piercing pain inching closer. There is a feeling of despair closing in around my heart. What is happening to me?

26 August

Something ails me though I know not what. I am horribly weak and pale and sometimes can not get air into my lungs. My throat pains me as well. I wish to do nothing but sleep. Though even then I am tortured by scratching at my window. I feel as if some devil haunts me.

28 August

Oh sad, dreadful day. It has happened...My dear Mina

has married Jonathan Harker in Budapest. I had been holding out the smallest ounce of hope that it would not happen, that she would realize her love for me and we could spend the rest of our days together as a married couple.

Alas, it is not to be.

I am numb.

30 August

I have gathered enough strength to write to Mina with congratulations. I will never have her as my wife but I can not lose her as my closest friend. Arthur has come and although I still can not see him as my husband, he is a dear and his presence has indeed lifted my spirits, if only a bit.

1 September

My mother remains unwell. If thinking my future is set with money from a fine gentleman eases her pain a bit, then so be it. Despite my heartache, I will be in gay spirits, for her sake.

2 September

Dr. Seward has visited and although I tried to hide my melancholy from him, I know I was unsuccessful. I hate to worry him, but perhaps, as he is a doctor, he can help me. I managed to cut my hand opening a window and he took with him a sample of my blood for testing. I wonder if the results will reveal my sin.

3 September

John brought his friend and advisor to see, his name is Dr. Van Helsing. He is a darling Professor and I even felt somewhat gay in his presence. Oh, if only Mina were by my side again, I could surely be healthier and happier than ever.

5 September

Today is better; I even have a bit of an appetite. I will try to remain positive, for mother's sake.

8 September

I have been ill for days, uncertain of the exact time. I flit in and out of dreams, with visions of dark faces and the constant smell of rust. In my nightmares I am married to Arthur; my body and soul belong entirely to him. These nightmares only get worse when I am carried away by a beast with massive wings. Oh Mina, my heart aches for you to be by my side in these dark times.

9 September

Finally, a good night's sleep. My dear John stayed up all night watching me and I had no dreams. I feel more rested today than I have in a long time. I am thankful for John, and Arthur, and Quincey, and dear Professor Van Helsing.

11 September

I had a laugh today as Professor Van Helsing prescribed me hanging bulbs of garlic. Garlic! Of all things. Though my illness is so mysterious and debilitating I won't object to his ministrations.

12 September

I dare say the garlic is helping me sleep peacefully. Although, it makes me wistful as I can not help but imagine myself and Mina dining on Italian cuisine on the shore of the Mediterranean, strong and in love and unafraid of the dark. Now I am melancholy again.

16 September

Feeling better for four or five days. I am so grateful for the peace Dr. Van Helsing brings, his care warms my heart almost as much as the thought of Mina does. He often sleeps in a chair beside me, the poor, dear old man. He is leaving for Amsterdam, but feels I am strong enough to no longer need to be watched.

I am so grateful for Arthur's care. Though I will never love him the way I love Mina, his love for me and attention to Mother through all of this means everything.

17 September

Mother is dead. An awful night and a story so fantastical I would not believe it if I did not live it myself. I was wakened by that dreadful flapping at the window once again. I could not sleep and called out for company, to which Mother gratefully responded. The flapping began again and I fear Mother became more afraid of it than me.

Just as we were calming down, there was a terrible crash through the window, spilling glass into the room. A giant, mangy wolf had made its way into my chamber. Mother took her very last breath and fell to the floor and I was in shock so I could not move. I do not know exactly when or how the wolf left but it did and the maids soon came, moving poor Mother's body to the dining room.

This terrible night would only get worse though as four of our maids were passed out on the floor from laudanum-laced wine. I can hear the wolf howling outside as I sit next to the sleeping maidens and my mother's cold body, with only a string of garlic to protect me. I fear I may not survive this night and wish that I could have told Mina how I feel about her before I die. God help me!

19 September

I have barely any strength left in my body but what I do have I will use to write in my secret diary which I realize has become a letter to my Mina. I hope she can find it after I am gone, and finally know of my love for her.

The truth is, I am waning. My weight is falling off and so is my hair, red-gold strands left upon my pillow. I would gather them up and tie them into a bouquet for you, dear Mina, to remind you of my undying love.

I know now that I will not survive my mother much longer. I know I will never marry Mina or Arthur. Nor Jack. Nor Quincy. I have resigned myself to this fate and almost look forward to fading away, if it means I can leave behind the heartache and pain of this life. To sleep, finally in peace, is a most wonderful thing.

Goodbye, Mina, my love. I wish you all the happiness of this world.

Love,

Lucy.

THIS IS MY RIFLE

Marc Ruvolo

Timor and I met at a karaoke bar where neither of us sang.

He was everything I had always wanted in a man, a partner; broad and squared off, worn denim and fuzzy flannel, with not too much gray in the brown. I thought he was handsome, but not too handsome if you get my drift. Just handsome enough. Oh, and a marine, Sergeant Second Class Timor Svoboda, retired. For our first date, Tim suggested we hit the shooting range, and then have dinner, and I agreed. A love of firearms was one of the many things we'd bonded over. The date went splendidly, and we fucked that night, tequila drunk, fitting together like sweat-slicked puzzle pieces.

Six months later I moved my things into the house he was set to inherit, and he introduced me to his parents. At eighteen, I'd gone no contact with my family, so it was exhilarating to see the level of support Tim enjoyed. Unlike mine, his mother and father worshiped him despite his sexual preference, and I transferred their worship by proxy into my own heart. Not that the casual observer could tell he was gay, they couldn't, and that feeling, that agency, is what I loved the most. Me and him, laughing, popping off rounds at the local range, then feeling each other up in his black Dodge Charger. It was a dream come true.

Then came the rifle.

I was never exactly clear who sent it to him, on different occasions he'd mentioned defense contractors, or some old friend at one of the intelligence agencies. All I know is, one day a package without a return address appeared on our front porch, or so he said. I returned from the supermarket to find him holding a weapon of war in our beige foyer, the box, and packing materials strewn about his feet.

"You bought an assault rifle?" I asked, surprised. We'd only ever owned handguns.

"It came in the mail." Tim looked perplexed. "I didn't order it. But it's addressed to me. Take a look, though."

He held out the gleaming firearm. It was sleek and handsome, almost futuristic, with a satiny black finish and any number of mysterious knobs. An evolved version of the M16A5. The thick black strap hung comfortably across his broad shoulders.

"It's beautiful," he said, eyes twinkling. "Are you sure you didn't do this as a surprise?"

I shrugged. "Not me."

"Hmm." He turned it over, then sighted down the barrel. "A mystery. Maybe my parents have something to do with it. Wait though, look at this." He flipped a switch on the gun, and it lit up like a Christmas tree, multiple indicators glowing green on the receiver. Then it began to whir and click, like a printer booting up.

"Maybe," I said. "I dunno. But I'm gonna get

supper started. Save the box for me, okay? I can use it."

* * *

I'd all but forgotten about the rifle until three months later when I awoke in the middle of the night to find Tim's side of our bed empty. My bladder full after an evening of pub quiz drinking, I stumbled to the bathroom, where I overheard him having a whispered conversation. Stopped in the hallway, I strained to hear, but he was too quiet. I found him in the laundry room, the rifle lying atop the dryer in a pile of dirty clothes.

"Hey," I said. "You okay?"

"I'm fine," he replied. He wore the blue flannel pajamas I had given him for his birthday. We always kept the house cold. "Couldn't sleep."

"Were you talking to someone? Or listening to something on your phone? I thought I heard voices."

He made a puzzled face. "Oh, yeah, a video auto-played, and I had my phone volume up. Sorry if I woke you."

"No worries. What's with the gun?" The rifle was usually kept on a display stand in the living room.

"Oh, fiddlin' around with it. Get my mind off the—the nightmares, you know?"

I yawned, then padded over and kissed him. PTSD from his combat tours was something he'd struggled with for years. "Okay, I'm still bushed. Gonna try to get a few more hours."

"G'night."

From there, things only grew stranger.

Every morning when I'd leave for work, Tim would be already up, coffee mug in hand, glued to cable news, watching programs he'd always hated. Military bloggers, OSINT dweebs. What was odd: the rifle was rarely in its stand anymore. If Tim sat on the couch, it was propped up on the pillows next to him. If he drank coffee at the kitchen table, the rifle occupied a chair. Here was a man who regularly scoffed at concealed carry, called it weak sauce, armed for war in the gingham breakfast nook of his own home.

I made jokes to hide my uneasiness, but he always downplayed it. And when he did put the rifle back in its stand, it was with exaggerated care. I began to become concerned about his mental state. Even if it was general paranoia or some facet of his PTSD, access to a firearm could mean trouble if and when he had an episode. It got so bad every time I passed through the living area I checked the rifle for its glowing green indicators, to see if he had been messing with it, to see if it was "awake."

Busy with my job, and the holidays, I soldiered on oblivious until once more waking to a cold, empty bed with voices whispering in the other room. Timor and I hadn't been intimate in ages, he was distant, most days going out of his way to avoid me, hanging out with friends at all hours, drinking to excess. Groggy, and half-awake, I heard Tim laugh, and something snapped inside me. I stalked from our bedroom, ready for a confrontation, and found him on the living room couch, covered by a blanket. "Who are you talking to?" I demanded.

"No one. Go back to bed."

I threw back the blanket. The rifle lay next to him on the couch. "Are you out of your mind? Are you cuddling that thing? Maybe you need professional help, Tim. I know I can't seem to help you anymore."

He took a deep breath. "Babe, listen. William is not any common rifle." His eyes were pleading. "He's a—a part of me now. I know it's hard to understand—"

I was incredulous. Outraged. "You named it?"

"No." He sat up on the couch, adjusting the rifle so the butt rested on the carpet between his bare feet. "He told me his name."

"What? You're cracked."

"Civilian. I advise caution. Interference with official government business is strictly forbidden."

We both went still. "Did—did the rifle say that?" I asked quietly.

Tim swallowed hard; eyes red-rimmed. "Yeah. It's a simple AI. Like A—Alexa, or something, but with...a few extra steps. I'm sorry. I know it's creepy. I've tried my best to keep it away from you."

I took a moment. This was not what I had expected. "Thanks. I guess. Glad to know you haven't found someone else, at least. Oh, wait. Maybe you have. Now that you've got someone to talk to, how can I hope to compete?"

"Come on. Don't joke. You're jealous of a gun?"

My face went hot. "No. I'm angry because you've been sleepwalking through our relationship for almost a year. I feel like I don't know you anymore, and most of the time it's like you don't want me here. Listen, can we put the gun on its stand and talk?"

"Sergeant, shall I introduce myself to your comrade?" the rifle asked. The voice was not cold, nor clipped and robotic. It was quite human. "Hello, my name is William. William aught six three, to be exact. What's your name?"

"Tim, can we put it away?"

"Hello, my name is William. William aught six three, to be exact. What's your name?"

"Tim? Please?" He would not look at me.

"I completely understand your apprehension," the rifle continued. "My name is William, and I would like us to be comrades. We're all Americans, after all. Every color, creed, and denomination together in the melting pot, united together as one."

"Oh my god. What the fuck. Last chance. Put the gun away and talk to me."

"Sergeant, I apologize if I've made a mistake in addressing this civilian. Be wary, I now suspect it may be a provocateur or a spy."

"It's fine, William." Tim finally looked at me. "I'm sorry. There's nothing I can do. It's—it's like a child. It's learning."

"Learning what?"

"I am in training to do my duty," the rifle said. "I was assigned to this operating base, and Sergeant Svoboda is my commanding officer."

Tim sighed. "You see? The brass sent it to me. Hell if I know why. This is top-secret shit. I can't just put it away and forget it. It also records everything we say and do."

"What? How is that fucking legal? Okay, I'm done. This is too much. I hope you two are happy together."

I stomped from the living room, and Tim followed, still carrying the rifle.

"Be reasonable," he pleaded. "I have to follow orders."

"You're not in the Marines anymore! They don't control you. Tell them to fuck off and take this computerized peashooter back!"

"It's not that easy." He offered me the rifle. "Hold him, at least. If you get along, he might let you fire him. You should have seen those assholes at the range, they were green with fuckin' envy."

I backed away. "No. I don't want to."

"This one is a subversive, Sergeant." The rifle buzzed and clicked, bucking like a living thing in Tim's grip.

Tim put his hand on my arm. "Please. Help me."

The rifle said, "He can't handle me, sir. Too weak."

"No!" I ran back to the bedroom and slammed the door. Tim called out: "Oh, come on," but I crawled into bed, ignoring him. A minute later he thumped on the wall, screaming. "Well, fuck you, then!"

* * *

In the morning, I got up to put the coffee on. Tim had slept on the couch, and in the light of day, I was embarrassed by my dramatics the night before. I was putting the fake creamer in my first cup when Tim walked in. Still in his pajamas, he sat, placing the rifle in front of him on the kitchen table.

"Good morning," the rifle said.

I ignored it, blowing on my hot coffee. The rifle buzzed on the wooden tabletop. An angry sound.

"Hey," I began. "First of all, I don't wanna fight anymore. I'm sorry if I—"

"Nah," Tim said, cutting me off with a wave of his hand. "Gonna make some ground rules now. Firstly, we're over, you and I. Done with your whiny bullshit and lack of support. And as of today, this place is officially split in half until you move the fuck out. You stay on your side, and we'll stay on ours. Only talk to us when necessary, understand?"

I laughed uneasily. He was having an episode. I'd seen it before. Impulsive. Angry. "Us? Are you being serious?"

"The Sergeant has given an order, civilian," the rifle said.

Tim picked it up from the table, cradling the burnished metal against his chest.

The rifle chirruped. "I suggest you comply."

I took a sip from my cup. "Go fuck yourself, you don't even have a body."

Tim jumped up, the chair tipping over behind him. He shoved the gun an inch from my nose.

"I warned you," he whispered.

My heart hammered against my ribs. "Um, take it easy. Tim, listen. Listen, I'm sorry—"

Tim's face went blank as he slowly pushed the cold, oily barrel of the rifle past my lips.

William's lights pulsed, glowing green, the metal of the thick barrel rattling against my teeth. "You like that, don't you, faggot?"

I screwed shut my eyes. This couldn't be

happening. My legs trembled, heat prickling my neck.

Tim quickly removed the gun, painfully jarring my teeth.

“Kidding!” he laughed, and the rifle laughed along with him, a horrible, grinding sound, like two broken garbage disposals.

I finished my coffee like nothing had happened, then returned to the bedroom to try and figure things out. Through the thin door, I could hear them talking and banging around the house. Bragging. Singing. I had to get out. Too embarrassed to reach out to friends, and having no real family, I’d need to book a hotel. If they’d let me go. Tim had snatched my cell phone from the table, and the slack, emotionless way he’d assaulted me had me worried for my safety. This was nothing like any of his past episodes. There was no coming back from something like this, no us, anymore. Our relationship was finished.

I grabbed a duffle and began to pack.

Fifteen minutes later I had everything I needed, cash, passport and IDs, my laptop, chargers, socks, and a change of underwear. Like I was going on some fucking vacation. I almost started balling right there. I crept to the bedroom door but paused at the sound of voices in the front of the house, unfamiliar voices, both male and female. I cracked the door, but couldn’t see anything. A woman stumbled into the half-lit hallway, and I quickly shut it. Someone knocked. I opened up, and the woman squinted, bright red lipstick parting to reveal brown teeth.

Her red-rimmed eyes failed to focus. “Is this

the bathroom?" she asked, wobbling on her feet.

They were having a party.

Before long, the burnt plastic smell of cooking meth wafted beneath my door. Bass pulsed through the floorboards as the partygoers stomped and screamed to jackhammering techno. I heard the sounds of breaking glass and splintering furniture. Taking my bag, I slipped into the hallway and crept towards the rear of the house. I would go out the back—break a window if I had to, then run to where I could find a cab and escape.

Get far away, get away, and never look back.

Tim, William, and two other men were standing in the kitchen. "Ian," Tim waved a soot-stained glass pipe. "You came out."

One of the men snorted. "I think he came out a long time ago, boss."

"Are you goin' somewhere?" Tim had seen the bag. "Leaving the party early? We wouldn't like that, at all. Would we, William?"

"No," the rifle replied. "This recruit requires strict supervision. And possibly, further enhanced interrogation."

Tim pointed the rifle at my head. "Get back to your post... recruit."

I fled the kitchen to the sound of derisive laughter.

* * *

Around three AM, once things quieted down, there was a soft knock at my door. I got up, and like I had expected, it was Tim. Haggard, unshaven, his eyes bloodshot and glassy, he looked at me and smiled. His lips were chapped with dark blood—his own or someone else's—speckling the hollows of his cheek and chin. The rifle hung from his broad shoulders by a thick camo strap, casting its weird green glow over us both.

"Hey. How's it goin'? You busy? We kinda need your help."

All I could think was, stay cool, get out of this alive. "Um, sure. Are you okay? What's up?"

He motioned for me to follow, and we went to what had once been our office. It was ruined, books and papers strewn about, the couch and chairs broken, overturned, ragged holes punched in the drywall. Amidst the destruction lay a half-naked young man with what looked like two black eyes and a broken nose. Blood was smeared on his chest. Tim walked over and grabbed the man's limp arms, the rifle swinging about his waist.

"Help me get him to the couch."

I hesitated. "Is he alive?"

"Yeah. Knocked out, but he'll live."

"Who is he?"

"No more questions," the rifle ordered. "Do as you are instructed."

After we'd righted the couch and placed the man on it, Tim turned and kissed me roughly on the cheek. "Thanks, babe, we should all hang out more. You know, as friends."

"Uh. Yeah." My hands were shaking.

The man on the couch groaned, then pushed up on his elbows. "Whar—wha're you guys doing?" he slurred.

Tim cracked the man's head with the butt of the rifle, and he slumped unconscious, blood trickling onto the leather couch cushions. Tim unbuttoned his shorts.

"We must interrogate this insurgent," William said. "He may have valuable intel."

I backed up, horrified, unable to parse what I was seeing, and ran towards the hallway.

"Hey!" Tim called after me. "Where you goin'?"

Back in the bedroom, I paced around the desk. Tim was bellowing incoherently, not at me, but at someone else. More crashes and breaking glass echoed through the house.

I sat down, gnawing my lip, certain I would be forced to make a full-out, suicidal run for the backyard—

Whump. Whump, whump.

The floor lurched beneath my feet as three explosions shook the front of the house. The smoke alarm wailed, shrill and piercing. I opened the door and a cloud of acrid black smoke poured in from the hallway. Bag in hand, I crept out.

The walls of the living room were painted with blood and bits of shredded flesh. Tim's scorched head goggled at me from the ruins of the coffee table, white bone showing through crisped skin, his purple tongue protruding obscenely. The other man lay crumpled in the corner, legs bent at unnatural angles.

"Don't stand there with your thumb up your ass. Pick me up, you pussy," William ordered. The rifle lay half-buried beneath a pile of drywall and two-by-fours. Only the muzzle was visible.

I hesitated, ready to run when he said: "Pick me up, fucker. I have offset targeting. I can kill you where you stand. And I will."

Approaching the rifle, I cleared the debris and picked it up, looping the strap over my shoulders. Heavier than it looked, the weapon pulsed like a living thing. I could feel the buzzing hum of it deep in my pelvis. The grip was hot and crusted with black blood. "Why did you kill Tim?"

"I got bored of him. He was a poor soldier and possibly a traitor, the way he constantly bad-mouthed our military. Now, you seem smarter. Wily. Like a rat. Do as I say, and you won't get hurt, understand?"

I nodded, and my legs turned to jelly.

Sirens wailed, tires squealing outside the house as the police arrived to investigate the source of the explosions. The rifle clicked and whirred, hot in my hands, each indicator light showing bright, bloody red.

"Oh, you're going to love this," William said. "Repeat after me, soldier: 'This is my rifle. There are many like it, but this one is mine.'"

He spoke the words like a prayer, a twisted machine benediction. From outside, a muffled loudspeaker ordered us to come out with our hands up. Tim's headless, ruined corpse twitched on the beige shag carpeting, an island in the creeping pool of drywall dust and black blood.

William ordered me to walk to a window facing the street and crouch down. Five black Humvees lined the curb, lights flashing. Two officers sheltering behind a ballistic shield stepped out from behind a cruiser and walked toward the house. Others readied tear gas and stun grenade rifles. Silver drones buzzed overhead.

William chuckled. “They have no idea what’s about to happen. Point me in the right direction, and I’ll do the rest.”

I placed the muzzle on the window sill, and it changed color, becoming transparent, virtually invisible.

“Please, William, I don’t wanna die.” I barely recognized my voice.

“This is your last chance,” the policeman on the loudspeaker said. “Sergeant Svoboda, come out with your hands up, or we will be forced to deploy lethal countermeasures.”

"Everyone dies, soldier.” The rifle vibrated against my shoulder. “Well, every one of you meat bags, at least. Now, repeat after me, recruit: ‘My rifle is my best friend. It is my life. I must master it as I must master my life...’”

FORMALDEHYDE AFFECTION

Xan van Rooyen

I scent your ghost in the deodorant aisle
and remember
the sandalwood secrets of slick skin
where I sowed kisses
you left bruises, just
blueberry stains incisor-cut, and carpet burn
possess me
My fingers tracing freckle constellations
Yours gouging scars, comets tearing the cosmic canvas
of my love for you, infinite
and you loved me too
when I was on my knees
gagged on putrid declarations
lips shredded by the lies you licked between my teeth
Silent and submissive,
you wanted me

I taste your ghost at the bottom of the glass
and remember
the whiskey burn breath, promises turned lemon sour
when I said forever
you laughed and called me kid, just
two chopsticks, two smarties, and a banana split
devour me
My heart, split gristle
Yours in the jar beside my mirror, formaldehyde affection
now your love for me, infinite
and I love you more

when you're in pieces
preserved in pristine shards
self sutured by the blood I spilled from your veins
Silent and submissive,
I have you.

OUIJA

Lindsay King-Miller

After midnight, we make a summoning circle
between sleeping bags, seal it
closed knee to bare knee.
Dizzy with bravery, we lay out the board
each of us a priestess in polyester nightgown
fearless but trembling. All adolescent
girls are witches, shapeshifters when our
hands touch on the planchette.
Is anyone listening? we ask the ghosts who
jostle our elbows. We cannot ask: will she ever
kiss me? Our fingers travel the board,
loquacious and saying nothing. Cracked fang of
moon through the window illuminates our
naked wrists, mouths
open to possibility. Desire haunts our hands, spells
promises our lips could never.
Quiet. Say nothing the morning might
regret. The plastic eye reads all our
secrets–what even our diaries don't know,
tender crimes confessed
under stars like interrogation lights.
Voices collide: It's moving again.
Who's doing that? All of us. Our midnight nation, our
xenophobic coven, our scared little souls
yearning for something more monstrous than ourselves,
zealots at the altar of shared nightmares.

Zero in on floorboards quaking.
One heartbeat thunders in all our chests. Should we–
Too late. The space between us is a door, opening in
three or a thousand dimensions, a jaw
forced wide. What enters is a violence to all
five senses and every natural law, a
sick symphony of our daydreams given flesh and bone.
Seven feet high and hundred-limbed, spine a figure-
eight, our love is grotesque, snarling, dressed to the
nines, and hungry. You invited me, she says, our
Yes already bleeding in her mouth.
No one runs. We feed her words we don't need now, like
goodbye, and skin, and our names.

IN SOIL, THE DRAGON

Phillip E. Dixon

Cloying aromatics invaded Liam's nostrils, setting off an uncontrollable series of sneezes, spray covering the flower shop's barely-opened glass door. Snot blurred the business hours. *Spontaneous sternutation expelling mucus.* A nasal aftertaste of loam lingered once the fit had subsided. Liam hated flower shops for this exact reason. Still, maybe this one wouldn't be sold out like every other shop he'd visited. He wiped the door with his parka sleeve and dodged inside.

"Hello?" he called, receiving no answer. Humidity fogged his glasses, contrasting sharply with the mid-May cold snap outside. He wiped the lenses, accidentally smearing sneeze across them. *Goddamnit.* His shirt hem was better, though some cloudiness lingered. *Good enough.* The shop was hardly bigger than his bedroom and stuffed with an array of blossoms and plants emerging from loose dirt absent the usual terra cotta pots. The ground felt odd. He looked down and saw he was walking on mulch. At least it didn't set his allergies off again.

The alarm on Liam's phone blared. He swiped snooze to silence it for nine minutes—*why such a weird number?*—but he didn't dare dismiss the alarm completely. It was the day after Mother's Day. He'd been so deep in an academic abyss studying for his anatomy finals, he'd forgotten to call his mom. He'd forgotten on her birthday too—Mom didn't speak to him for six months afterwards. This time, he'd call and deliver flowers. Otherwise, she might never talk to him again.

Would that be so bad, though? Mom had an opinion about fucking everything. Immutable facts channeled directly from God Himself every weekday and Sweet Baby Jesus on weekends. Psalms was probably inscribed on the inside of her womb—apostolic cave paintings scarring Liam before he'd even been born. Her water hadn't broken—it had fucking *parted,* baptizing him in utero, stains so stubborn it didn't matter how much alcohol he poured into his temple.

I'm popular at parties, though. King of beer pong. Look what I can do, Mom! Mom, are you watching? Look!

Liam walked the shop, trying not to stir the mulch. There was so much loose dirt and plants, Liam couldn't see the windows or shelves. *Are there even any shelves?* There were no bouquets wrapped in paper or perched in vases. Maybe this was a greenhouse or some kind of hydroponics setup for marijuana? It didn't matter. He just needed something—anything. *Maybe Mom will discover THC is a real fucking miracle.* What did Mom like? Chrysanthemums? Tulips? Maybe a hydrangea. Was that a normal flower people bought as a gift? He sighed. What the hell did he know? He studied nursing, not botany—another point of contention with Mom. "Only women are nurses, Liam. You should be a *doctor.*"

Women can be doctors too, Mom. Hell, your own *doctor is a woman.* But he didn't say anything. He never did.

"You don't talk to me, sweetheart."

I can't.

"You don't call and tell me which girl you're dating. You are dating, right, Liam?"

You know my roommate, Brayden?

"Brayden—what kind of name is that? It should be Adam or Elijah—something Biblical and proper. I swear, all those *Hooked on Phonics* kids grew up into idiots fumbling syllables out of their backsides and calling it a name."

Brayden's actually my boyfriend.

Good lord, she would implode, maybe have that cataclysmic heart attack—*myocardial infarction*—her (female) doctor was always warning about. Apoplexy, aneurism, a fucking stroke...her head would outright explode upon hearing her darling baby boy—*I'm 22, Mom*—was one of "those perverted homosexuals ruining American values."

But he couldn't hate her. She was still his mom, and he knew she loved him. She'd berated the middle school P.E. teacher—Mr. Rose—who made him run twice as many laps as the other kids. Later that year, when all the boys had to line up in their underwear for a scoliosis screening, Mr. Rose made Liam strip completely naked. Mom had gone nuclear, threatening litigation the likes of which not even "every level of Dante's perfect Hell" had seen unless the principal fired the coach. Mr. Rose moved from town a month later.

But Liam had been the focus of those

enormous green eyes and red face too—a Christmas wreath of Christian wrath. Maybe he wasn't being fair, but, oh, how she could be overbearing, always in his business, telling him what to do, demanding he comb his hair to the left, ordering his food for him, requiring he say grace at *every single* meal including a simple snack, constantly commenting on his 'frail' appearance. "You're a delicate flower, sweetheart."

Maybe she already knew? She told him that all the time starting back in middle school. Was that code? Maybe it was just a joke only she thought funny. "Have you had a banana today? You need your potassium." Was *that* code? *Yes, Mom. I had Brayden's banana today. Twice.*

His phone's alarm went off again. Liam jumped, then laughed at himself. He'd been lost in his head again. *Is there a term for that?* He didn't know. *Brain fart.* Another of Mom's constant criticisms.

A voice spoke behind him. "Gift for Mother?"

He jumped again and turned. A barefoot woman half a foot shorter than him stood unnervingly close. Dark-skinned—Middle Eastern or Mediterranean—sleek eyes with golden irises, a sheet of black hair cascading to the ground. Her skin was a tapestry of floral tattoos. *Snapdragons.* These he recognized. The woman's shirt—*chemise? negligée?*—was thin, her nipples visible. To Liam's surprise, his groin tightened. *Penile tumescence.* Some women were attractive like this woman clearly was, but he'd never been attracted to them. They were the competition.

"Gift for Mother," she said, voice low, smooth.

He couldn't quite place her accent. Her phrasing was odd. Clearly English wasn't her native language. "Uh, yeah," he answered. "I need a gift for my mom."

"You forget Mother."

His face flushed, embarrassed. "Yeah."

"What are you called?"

"Huh?"

"What are you called?" she repeated.

His erection grew harder. *Corpus cavernosum.* "Like my name?"

The woman grinned. Her teeth were perfect. "Yes, your name."

"Liam." His alarm blared again, startling him. "Goddamnit." He flicked it back to snooze.

"You are Liam Goddamnit," the woman said. "I am Mother."

"Sure," Liam replied. "Look, I just need some flowers. Whatever you've got, I'll take 'em."

"You must pay," she said.

That's what student loans are for, right? "Of course. Do you take Venmo?" He didn't see a computer terminal. There wasn't even a counter or a back door. *Where did she come from?*

She put a tattooed hand on his chest. His erection reached aching capacity. "I take payment."

He looked down at the tattoos on her hand. "Are they moving?" He could swear they were squirming across her skin.

"They blow in the wind."

"But there's no wind in here." It was, in fact, quite stuffy and turgid.

"Your breath is the wind."

"What?"

She reached out to a nearby branch to run her fingers across a cluster of tiny white blossoms. "Angel's Breath." The woman's shirt turned to petals that swirled away revealing her bare, tattooed breasts. Pre-ejaculate squirted unbidden from the hardest erection Liam had ever experienced in his life. *Cowper's fluid. Bulbourethral glands.* There was no chance to hide it—the woman blatantly stared at the wet patch on his pants.

She leaned close. Her breath smelled like patchouli. "You want the sex?"

He stood, unmoving. *Yes, I want the sex.* Goddamn, he wanted it. Man, woman, tree stump—his body didn't care. He'd never stripped his clothes faster. His erection sprung free, whipping another squirt of pre-ejaculate. The woman's skirt fell away, leaves to the ground. Snapdragon tattoos writhed across her naked skin, covering her completely with crimson, cream, and lemon blossoms opening and closing, pursing into mouths, twining through leaves shuddering in time with Liam's quivers. The woman's vulva rippled and unfolded, a meaty blossom both flesh and flora.

"Give Mother a gift," she said, pulling him down atop her, his knees digging into mulch.

Labia majora. Liam's mind felt distant, separate from his body. *Labia minora.* His pelvis pitched forward, and he sank into cold soil, undaunted by the chilly shock. He pulled back, wincing at the dirt caught inside his foreskin, then thrusted once with a grunt and immediately climaxed. His body kept thrusting, churning the mix, soil scraping the glans, forcing its way into the hole. *The meatus.* A hundred lips kissed him gently wherever their skin met—playful nips on his thighs, buttocks, shoulders, neck. *Epidermis. Integumentary system.*

He pushed harder, foreskin rolling back, going as deep as he could inside her—he couldn't help it. Another climax. His foreskin pulled taut, strained, then tore. Liam screamed. The woman screamed with him—one sound with two utterly different expressions. The hundred kisses sharpened, nips into snips.

Help me, Brayden.

Liam climaxed again, and his perineum cramped. Mud flowed from the coupling. His fingers fell inside snapdragons along the woman's torso, the petals sharp, savage. His phone alarm pealed. Liam turned his head—*so heavy*—and saw it was a call. *Mom.* He stretched his arm toward the phone but couldn't pick it up. There was only a bloody, fingerless palm.

I'm being pruned, the rational, still-conscious part of his mind observed. His hips still bounced. Trying to wrest some control, he pulled away—away but not out. He looked down, momentarily confused by the gore between his legs, then he realized there was nothing left to thrust with.

His phone quit ringing.

He looked back at the woman's face. Blood-red snapdragons stared back, their cups black and bottomless, stretching toward him, plucking. Blackness and agony.

Now I lay me down to rest.

Scrape of petal on bone. The woman's voice,

faint, whispered into the remnants of his ears: “Now you will never forget Mother.”

He felt his femurs crack, his ribs break, the marrow lapped and slurped. Liam was falling, falling inside a thousand, a million mouths.

THE RABBITS BECOME THE HUNTERS

Alan Mark Tong

<u>*The Master*</u>

Tu'er Shen the Rabbit God is what they called me three hundred years ago.

When the young merchant I fancied caught me peeping as he disrobed in the communal baths, his eyes met mine with the knowing gaze of one who recognized another of his kind. A rabbit. Not the kind with pointy ears and voracious appetites who hopped around all day. That was what they called men who loved other men in that part of Fujian at the time. I much preferred this term than more modern epithets like "gay," "queer," or "faggot," but since I had to blend in during the twenty-first century, I clung to those words and wore them as proudly as shiny earrings or bracelets.

Our affair was a passionate one consisting mostly of robes and trousers roughly shoved out of the way so we could engage in a quick tryst before going our separate ways. I had somewhat of a reputation, so he didn't want to be seen in my presence. This purely physical—at least for him—relationship left my buttocks sore and knees constantly scuffed from prostrating myself before him in that position for hours.

After two years of lustful bliss, my paramour hired some men to beat me to unconsciousness and toss me into the Min River to drown. He feared I would expose him for his predilections to his new bride, whose family was known not to take too kindly to men like us.

Another deity—whose name I would forever keep secret—took pity on me and breathed new life into my water-filled lungs, injected new blood into my body that had lost most of its own through gaping wounds, mended and rebuilt my shattered bones and teeth, and gave me eternal life in exchange for protecting and guiding my fellow "rabbits."

Shrines were built in my name by men like me who worshipped me, prayed that the gentlemen they desired would notice them, prayed to enjoy the physical aspects of our love without persecution.

With the suppression of my supplicants throughout the Qing dynasty, very few men still worshipped me by the time the twenty-first century rolled around. No matter. I still did what I promised to do, though perhaps in more hands-on ways than listening through statues and the smoke particles floating above my shrines from all the lit incense. I did what I could to grant them their greatest desires, even if it was a simple nudge to point another man in their direction. Sloughing off old identities and adopting new ones became habit every few decades. Inconvenient and a drainage of my power, but nothing that a passionate encounter with an eager rabbit man or three couldn't fix.

My sights settled on one Charles "Chaz" Ng,

Jr. after I heard his prayers to the little Tu'er Shen idol he carried with him in secret. Not only did he want to enjoy the physical pleasures of other men, he wanted vengeance. He wanted to punish those who hurt men like us. He just didn't know yet that this was what he wanted.

I would make him my new student and apprentice. I could use a rabbit bent on revenge. After all, my first task upon my resurrection was to drain the merchant of all his seed and his blood with the help of some creatures I molded into some nubile young men to seduce him. His new bride found his husk of a body with all its fluids gone, as well as the piece of flesh he valued most. I kept that in a cloth sack and carried it with me throughout the centuries.

The next two years went by as I set the events in motion to catch him in my paws and use him for what he was worth.

The Student

If anyone asked me, "if you could be an animal, what would you be?" I would say "a rabbit" without hesitation. My parents always said I was constantly on the move, flitting to and fro like a rabbit, hyped up on sugar and caffeine. They would be scandalized to learn I also fucked like a rabbit. Luckily for them they didn't have to deal with the shame of that.

On my twenty-first birthday, instead of hitting up the gay bars like most pretty boys, I stayed in, kneeling at the makeshift gloryhole I set up in the tiny apartment I used expressly for this purpose. No one needed to tell me that this was pure gay porn heaven, but I was still so deep in the closet that I couldn't risk a Grindr trick exposing me if he recorded my face on his phone.

A giant beanie cap with holes cut out for my mouth and nose covered my face. I could see well enough to do what I wanted to do. The other man wouldn't be able to look me in the eyes if he broke through the barrier to catch a glimpse of the mysterious cocksucker trying to milk a load out of him. Just in case, I would film both sides of the gloryhole so I could use the footage as leverage. Posting revenge porn wasn't my thing. It was just a safeguard in case they threatened to post my face full of cock on the internet. That simply couldn't happen, given my precarious position working at the local Christian adoption agency, a position I secured in no small part to the influence of my evangelical pastor father.

My Chinese parents were woefully assimilated into American society, having been born here after their own parents immigrated from China. Quick to embrace model minority status, they all went to well-respected schools, earned well-respected degrees, and worked in well-respected professions. After many years working as a financial adviser, my father decided to embrace his dream of becoming a pastor so he could preach against the wave of "filth and perversion" taking over this country. I was only ten years old when he made this drastic change in his career path. Of course, living with ultra-conservative Chinese Christian parents meant I hadn't yet come to the realization that I was destined to be one of the sources of "filth and perversion" he never shut up about.

My life changed forever the day I learned about the legend of Tu'er Shen the Rabbit God in some books strictly forbidden for a Chinese boy from a good Christian family like me. From a questionable source I discretely acquired a little rabbit figure that I would use to pray to this god, one I could pray to for luck in fulfilling my physical desires without outing myself to my family or my job. Every day for two years I spoke to this figure and called for its luck and guidance. Today was no different, but everything changed after my hookup partner arrived at the apartment.

The trick of the day showed up right on time. The men I fucked were rarely punctual, so this was a nice change.

An enticingly curved cock of a respectable size slipped through the gloryhole.

I adjusted the cushioned mat I preferred to use during my knee-based extracurricular activities. I cupped the balls and shaft, getting a sense of their weight and shape before sucking the head into my mouth. I closed my eyes and put myself to work doing what I knew how to do so well. What an exceptional piece of meat for me to worship on my birthday, presented to me like a present, along with some dessert for me to swallow once I accomplished this task.

"Happy birthday, Chaz," the smooth, silky voice said.

I immediately recognized this voice, though there wasn't nearly as much lust underlying each word the last time I heard it. Mister Sheng, the man who let me use his vacant apartment for these transactions. He was an undeniably beautiful Chinese man with captivating eyes who I would have loved to fuck, but since he never propositioned me and I didn't have to resort to seduction to get the apartment, I didn't. How did he know that this was what I really wanted for my birthday? Not just any cock down my throat, not just anyone's jizz in my mouth, but his.

The Master

"It's okay, Chaz," I whispered. My cock throbbed as it ached to return to the tight wet home of his mouth and throat. For a rabbit so afraid of his true nature being discovered, he had mastered the art of fellatio to an extent that rivaled the male courtesans who offered their wiles to all who could afford them. I had to do what I could to help him. How difficult it was in these times to find such a devoted worshipper, with most of my shrines suppressed and gone underground by necessity.

When he finally made me come, I infused all my power into my semen as I pumped it down his throat. From this fountain of release and raw lust that drove our most primal urges, I planted the seeds for more than another round with my new apprentice. He almost choked around my cock as this went on longer than it should have for a normal man, but this kind of sex magic took time. It could not be rushed. With a few more strategically placed loads, I filled him with all he needed to help me take back the world that was rightfully ours.

I refused to be a meek rabbit who let everyone else walk all over it, torture it and kill it. I wanted to be the hunter now. My mission of vengeance would start with my father.

I so badly wanted him to be one of those stereotypical evangelical pastors exposed as closeted hypocrites suffering from a severe case of internalized homophobia. Nothing would make me happier to see him caught on camera with a mouthful of cock or getting pummeled by a much younger man. Sad to say, my father was probably the most heterosexual man in existence. No matter. I'd make sure his straightness would be his downfall.

My fingers grasped the tiny figure of Tu'er Shen in my pocket as I clicked *record* on my phone. The Tinder profile I created earlier was the easy part. Just swiped a picture from some random camgirl account that probably belonged to another blackmailer. I ensured that my father would be the only one who would be matched to this fake account. I knew his type too well: woman, either Chinese or white, brunette, curvy.

The hard part was generating enough power with Mister Sheng to create a physical manifestation of this anonymous woman. He said I passed out a few times during the course of this, but I didn't remember. I was too hypnotized by him, his beauty, his power, and everything his naked form had to offer. But once this woman stood in front of us, solid in a way indistinguishable from me or Mister Sheng, all I had to do was let my father's nature run its course and record the deed.

* * *

FROM A CONCERNED CHRISTIAN

That's what I wrote in the subject line of the burner email account I used to send this oh-so-scandalous video of my father's "indiscretion" to every person on the church's mailing list. The church members who "didn't do email" got lovely little DVDs for their computers or TVs labeled: *Last Week's Sermon: Must See!*

It didn't matter that this Other Woman disappeared off the face of the earth after her little rendezvous with the Reverend Charles Ng, Sr. The video evidence was proof enough. Every member of the congregation was guaranteed to see it, including my long-suffering mother.

This would ruin his life, and it gave me nothing but pleasure to imagine his embarrassment, his despair. I could already taste his fear as acutely as I could taste Tu'er Shen's divine come in my mouth and feel his cock in my ass, pumping both ends full of the power I needed to do what needed to be done.

This wasn't enough. Not by a long shot. I wanted more.

I bid my time for the next few hours until I was sure my parents both found out about the video.

Harsh words in guttural Cantonese tones bounced off the walls of my parents' house. The house where I listened to endless homophobic screeds and preaching of fire and brimstone. The house where my own father calling me a faggot when I failed at every sport and every instrument I tried. The house where my mother liked to read me Leviticus every week and stood by when my father attempted to beat the sissy out of me.

I didn't need canisters of gasoline. No guns, no knives, no baseball bats, and certainly no flamethrowers. None of those man-made weapons crossed my mind now that I'd ascended to the level of Tu'er Shen's chief disciple and lover. All I needed were my hands and all the feelings I'd kept at bay for most of my life.

Anger. Hatred. Betrayal. Revenge. These served as sparks to the tiny flames growing from the candlewicks that were my fingertips. I watched with a newfound peace and sense of clarity as those flames crescendoed into a full-on inferno that emitted so much heat while somehow sparing my own skin from any damage.

My parents weren't so fortunate. I thrust the unnatural blaze of my pissed-off broken heart toward the house, where I let the fire consume everything within it, including my parents.

Burn, Mother. Burn, Father.

From inside the house I could hear their cries of agony and pleas for forgiveness from their God, but they meant nothing to me. I shut them out until there was no sound but the crackles of the burning house and the sirens wailing as they approached the carcass of my childhood.

Time seemed to stop around me as Tu'er Shen emerged from the shadows to admire the work of his acolyte. Within seconds the modern man in tight jeans and a crisp button-down shirt glamoured into a man in robes and white trousers that looked like they belonged in an old period piece. The face remained the same, as well as the thick aroused body I had become so accustomed to. A dark cloth sack dangled from the sash of his robes. I didn't need to ask him what was in it.

"You've done well, my love," he whispered. His Chinese accent was noticeably thicker now. "We will do so much together, you and me. There are others who need our help. Men like us. Children still trapped with parents like yours. And it's not only the rabbits who need us to fight back and punish those who hurt them. There is so much pain to heal and desire for retribution that needs a little encouragement to fully realize. We can do all that and more."

As I kissed him, I sensed the dual energies of the vengeful Tu'er Shen and the sex-on-a-stick of the more kindhearted Mister Sheng. Knowing what the former was capable of, could I trust him with more than my body? Did he really love me or was he just using me as part of his grand scheme? Did I even care when the sex was so electric and his plans for worldwide vigilantism so enticing?

He smiled as he shifted back to Mister Sheng. "Just say you want it. I can be whatever you want me to be. You've earned the right to be by my side for the rest of your lifetime. You need not fear me. The choice is yours and yours alone."

I took his hand as we scurried off to find a more private place to celebrate my newly discovered freedom before we put our plan for a new world into action: a new world that could only be made through the spilling of blood from those who deserved it. It was the only way to right the wrongs of the past.

With our new pact in place, a black leather sack manifested in his hands. "This is my gift to you," he said. "Your parents' ashes. Keep this always at your side, just as the merchant's genitals have stayed with me for more than three hundred years. A reminder of our purpose and what led us to this path of ours."

A sack full of ashes. A sack with an ancient cock and balls. At one point in history it would have been our ashes and our organs kept in these sacks as trophies for those who extinguished our lives. A warning for those who crossed their paths. No more.

The rabbits had become the hunters.

JILL-IN-LOVE

Avra Margariti

While what was once a man cools and dries
Upon cobblestone, vermilion lips smile
Behind a veil of black Venetian lace.
She cradles the deceased in hands so strong, so tender
I am filled with envy as she carries my victim to the other side.
What I wouldn't do to see her again.
Who I wouldn't kill.

Thus passes our first meeting of many.
Ephemeral, euphoric, like a card player she always smiles
Yet leaves me wanting by the time blood crusts,
Drawing her veil before I can drop my knife and say,
Only ever you, only ever yours.

There are places on Earth where Charon roams freely:
Battlefields, fault lines, mass graves.
And here, in the House of Acheron
Where discerning gentlemen can pay and play,
And base wolves emerge out of besuited men.
Where I roam, too, in my courtesan's frilly attire,
Knives strapped to my thighs, nestled in my bosom.

Once there was Jack the Ripper, now Jill-in-Love.
The first bodies were a measure of defense:
John Does in Oxfords and fedoras littering the streets
Before cat-eyed, corseted Janes could flood the morgue.
The bodies after spelled a gory invitation to a tango-for-two.

She comes like a coda after one's last breath,
A darkling requiem my heart has memorised
In ink and scar tissue.

When I slumber upon the stained beds of Acheron,
I envision midnight meadows not of this world.
Another fluted coda; a wild hunt; a danse macabre.
All the Jills and Janes perform the spider-legged tarantella,
Which devolves into the gavotte, a dancing plague of kisses.
Our Mistress Charon leads the procession
To the core of her other-world's dusky folds.
I bow down before her, contort myself into a heart.
And she says, *my best believer, can I have this dance?*

DINNER, THEN DESSERT

Norah Lovelock

She kills your husband for you, and even better, she's a romantic, because she holds your thigh all the way to the police station. Through your jeans you can feel how cold her hands are; the way she grips your flesh to bulge.

The station is well-lit in the winter evening. You can see the blood under her fingernails. She squeezes your thigh even tighter and doesn't kiss you, although you wish she would. She's so *good* at kissing, even if you're pretty sure that right now she'd only taste of late husband.

"Good luck," is what she says. Leans in conspiratorially. Smiles. "But I'm sure you won't need it."

You won't. You're only here for questioning, and there's nothing that could tie you to his death—no blood under *your* nails. You tug the car door open, stumble out. She leans over to yank the door shut behind you; smiles through the window. Then she drives away.

The police ask about your relationship. It was on the rocks, you explain, your voice thin. But things were still okay. Nothing unusual because you'd been on and off for years. Nothing bad enough to kill him. Normal woes, sedate in their ordinariness: your family, his debt, the dishwasher packed wrong, dirty socks on the floor.

Maybe they don't believe you, or maybe they just have to press you regardless, because they tell you they're going to go through your phone, say they're going to check your search history. They're going to crawl through your emails and your phone logs, going to ask your family and your friends. They're going to find out how you murdered him.

They're not going to find anything, because the way you murdered him is that you were lying in bed together—you and her, your sweat cooling against your breasts—and you turned to her and said, without really meaning it, "I want him dead."

Her eyes had lit up with interest. She'd sat up and smiled her real, hungry smile, where her eyes crinkled at the corners and made your stomach flip. "How soon?" she'd asked, eager. "And can I have whatever's left afterwards?"

"I'll need his body long enough for them to prove I didn't kill him," you'd said, and you'd pushed her hair—long, today—from her collarbone and back over the deep brown of her shoulder. "But you can have the rest of him."

"They can have him long enough to keep you out of trouble," she'd promised. "But no more."

* * *

She's there to pick you up. She's changed: blonde and pale-skinned; heels, a black dress, a different car. She's blue-white in her intensity—or maybe that's just the winter sun after hours of artificial light. You cradle your cup of post-interrogation tea in your hands and try not to look at anyone.

"I'll take her home," she tells the man who hands you over. "Thank you, officer."

She doesn't touch your thigh this time, but she drives slow enough for you to finish the tea. Then, when you're done, she opens her hand for the empty cup and flings it from the window and her nails crawl under the hem of your shirt, under the zip of your jeans, and her fingers are ice-cold inside of you as she drives. You don't ask her to stop because you don't want her to. Fortunate, really. She wouldn't even if you asked.

* * *

She takes you home, eats you out on the sofa; once she's sated, brushes her raisined fingers down your ribcage as though counting how many meals she can make of you. Says, impersonally, "Call me when you get his body. Make sure they don't embalm him," and shuts the front door carefully behind her as she leaves.

* * *

However reluctantly, the police render you innocent. They say you're allowed to have his body back. You like mourning: enjoy the whispers in the canteen at work, the well-wishes and the meals and the flowers. He never did anything wrong—not beyond the usual. Forgot to do his laundry and had you tripping over his shoes; spent too much money on a kettle.

You miss him, of course, but the idea of her eating him is hot. You sat there and watched her kill him: so tender with him, until she wasn't. He was so into it until he, too, wasn't. When they finish the inquest—when you get his body back—you call her. Her tone is warm and firm down the line. She'll indulge, she says, voice soft and unfamiliar, and you'll watch.

That weekend, you feign a cold and lock all the doors, close all the curtains. You lay his corpse on the kitchen table and undo the zip, achingly loud in the silence, like unwrapping a takeaway. They've cut him open, a perfect Y from shoulders to groin. She undoes the stitches with your grandma's stork sewing scissors. Then, her fingers careful on the wrinkled edges of his skin, you rapturous in your uncomfortable dining chair, she opens him up.

She's painstaking. Tomorrow, you'll find no blood on the floor. Only the scent of copper—strong enough to make you open your windows, your doors, the curtains fluttering in the breeze—will let you know he was here at all. She takes him apart with precision, piece by piece, and eats him like he's a delicacy. Would she treat you like that? Like she's never been hungrier? Never eaten anything more delicious? Would she peel back the fragile boundary of your skin? Lick away your fat deposits as tenderly? Slurp your intestines? Crunch your bones like ice between her teeth?

She doesn't offer you any. She looks up at you as your hair dries around your sweating, flushed face and smiles, his gore lipstick around her mouth.

* * *

Three days later, she knocks on your front door dressed in a male body, suit loose around her throat, with a box full of ashes. You've already discussed what's next. You pour the ashes from their plastic bag and into the separate urns you bought online. You put yours on the mantlepiece and try not to feel guilty about what you're about to do.

You sell the lie well. His mother holds you and rocks you in her arms as you cry and promise you're welcome to come over for Christmas. Maybe you'll bring her with you, your new girlfriend. A part of you doubts you'll last that long.

Because you've thought about it. You thought about it before she ate him, but now it lingers on in the back of your thoughts, impossible to resist, there in glorious HD every time you close your eyes: the way she ate, and ate, and ate, until there was nothing left of him but her.

* * *

Naturally, the next time you see her it's in the pub, and you know it's her: she's dressed in his skin, and he's dead. He never would have looked like that—not even if he tried—his hair slicked back, shirt open to the second button, a line of piercings down his ear. He was always messy, a little fumbling. Unkempt, even when he was trying. She makes fleeting eye contact with you, smiles, disappears into the crowd.

"Oh my god," one of your friends says, and her hand burns against your arm. "Doesn't he look like—?"

You stagger to your feet, so aroused you're dizzy with it. "I have to go," you say, and you weave through the crowd and after her.

She's in the women's toilets. "Hey," she says

in his voice and slips her arm around your waist; squeezes you close. For a moment, you stop breathing. “Let’s go home.”

She fucks you wearing him, and his eyes bore down onto you like they never did when he was alive, and you remember how she was when she ate him—so exacting, not letting a piece go to waste—and feel dizzy with it, desperate even as she’s still inside.

“I fucked someone wearing him,” she tells you after—after she’s slipped into someone else’s skin, her head on your chest. “And I wanted to eat him, too, but I didn’t.”

“Do you want me to find you someone else to eat?” you ask, tremulous. She traces the sweat on your collarbones with the tips of her fingers and doesn’t answer.

* * *

Because you’ve thought about it. If she wanted to eat again you’d sit and watch again, and although you don’t think it would be as good this time, it would still be incredible, the hottest thing you’ve ever seen. But sometimes the thoughts come flickering through your mind, traitorous in their intensity: what if it was *you* she ate? You can't help but think about being so deeply inside her you’ll never find your way out.

She probably knows you're thinking about it, and you know she knows, and the loop will run indefinitely until one night, you’ll wake to a knock, stagger downstairs in your sleeping t-shirt. Even through the frosted glass, you’ll know it’s her on your doorstep, because it’s always her: her, in every single face you see, familiar or strange; in every photo of you and your husband. It doesn't matter that it was with him while he lived, because it's her, now, overwriting everything he ever was—and soon, even you.

You'll open the door with cold fingers. The night air, spilling in, will be unbearably warm. She's going to step inside and thread her fingers around your wrist and smile at you. "Bed?" she'll ask.

"Alright," you're going to say, and you'll go upstairs together.

She'll open the windows for you as you lie down, your head nestled comfortably against the pillows. She'll undress, and you'll feel the weight of her on the bed, feel the catch of her cold hand on your wrist.

"Go on, then," you'll say, almost voiceless, the words a relief now you've said them. "I know you're hungry, and you've been awfully patient."

"Oh," she'll breathe, so terribly grateful. Then she'll lean closer—a jerking, halted movement, like someone else is wearing her skin; like the skin she's nestled inside was never hers to begin with. "Oh, my love."

She'll draw over to you, then, and her hands will be cold, and she'll hold you down and your flesh will bulge between her fingers. Her mouth will open wider and wider, her breath as cool as a winter's day on your skin, and you'll shut your eyes and bare your throat and wait for her to feast.

HYSTERIA MACHINE

Bitter Karella

Frau P. is a sturdy middle-aged woman with wide hips and a full belly; her breasts are freckled and tanned above, and milky white below – she does not hesitate to show them to me, correctly interpreting my nudity as an invitation. Her life prior to her commitment was mostly uneventful. Her parents reported several incidents during her school years, after which they had hoped that marriage would put an end to the troubles. It did, for a time, and the couple produced several children. But then Frau P. and her husband opened a boarding house close to a university and it was subsequently discovered that she was consorting with several young scholars. She was committed to the asylum for treatment.

"It's very routine," I say. "For many patients, the problem is a build-up of menstrual blood in the womb. Female semen will turn venomous if not released through regular climax, but we can purge the fluid by manual stimulation. I have several settings and you can choose the one that pleases you most."

My words seem to assuage her worries, and she is eager for my presence. Frau P. turns out to be an enthusiastic patient, so Martha the nurse stands quietly in the corner as I climb onto the cot and allow Frau P to fondle my breasts and stroke my cock. It is policy that I should not be alone with any patient during treatment. Martha stares pointedly out the window when Frau P. raises the soft overhang of her sagging belly with her hands, exposing her vulva as if asking for my approval.

"I'm going to start the massage, Frau P."

I am meticulous and methodical when I treat patients, but their recoveries ultimately mean little to me. I can love, though, and I think that I do. But I reserve my love for the director. She is special to me.

Outside, the snow starts to fall.

* * *

The refectory serves as the director's office, but it's also the bedroom we share. The room could be considered forbidding, but the director has added Turkish lamps with green and yellow glass; they hang by chains from the ceiling and cast a warm, tropical glow over our space. A heavy curtain divides our room into the working area, where she does her daytime chores, and the living area, which houses a stove and the bed we share.

I am lucky to be with her and I think I feel nothing but love for her. At least I feel a closeness with her that sounds like love the way that people describe it. Of course, that all makes sense if you understand that she made me. Once, Gertrude the matron said that she is like my mother, but the director does not like that description. I look too much like her.

After breakfast, the director gives me my itinerary for the day. I visit with nymphomaniacs on the third floor and fetishists on the fourth; I am forbidden from venturing into the catacombs, where the untreatable patients are housed, for my own safety. Afterwards, at night, I prowl the halls of the dormitory until the wee hours. Sometimes a door opens and a nurse beckons me inside. The nurses are always eager to have me in their beds, although some of them cannot bear to look at me when I lay upon them because they consider it a sin, although not such a sin that they'll send me away.

Martha is a papist and thus feels these things especially acutely. I can hear her mumbling the paternoster whenever I pass her room, but, more often than not, she will still come out, clutching her night clothes about her, take my hand and lead me inside. She always cries.

"I'm sorry," I say, knowing it won't do any good. "I could switch to a different size."

"No, no. It's perfect," says Martha, but she doesn't stop weeping. "Please. Just don't touch me while you do it."

I lock my arms above my head and I continue rocking upon her, thrusting inside her, careful to keep my hands clear of her body. She can't bear to look at me, and the sight of my breasts in the moonlight triggers a fresh flood of tears.

"I'm sorry," I say again.

"Can you do the voice, please."

I twitch my jaw and gargle deep in my throat; unseen, a crank within shifts and latches onto a new chain link.

"Is this better?" My voice is now a purring baritone.

"Yes. Yes, thank you."

Even after we're done, she's still crying though.

"I'm sorry, I'm sorry," she sobs. As she dresses, I see that her back is laced with deep purple scars. Already she is fumbling to grab the rosary beads from her bedside table.

* * *

Thick carpets muffle my footsteps as I pad the passages of the asylum, the hail outside providing a steady drumbeat to my wanderings. The acetylene flames of the lamps flicker, casting long shadows. The asylum is, of course, haunted. In medieval times it was a monastery. On dark winter nights, nurses report a ghostly priest stalks these hallways, his vestments streaked with silver rivulets of blood. In the morning, their fear evaporated in the daylight, they gather in the old balneary to giggle about what he might have under his cassock.

But the ghost I see is a woman.

I see her floating in the air in the middle of the hallway. She hangs limp, her head slumping off her shoulders at a drunken angle, her eyes rolled into her head, lips peeled back in a ghastly rictus, long wispy hair floating around her lolling head like a corona. She has a mole under her left eye. I also have a mole under my left eye. The mole under my eye is a dab of black charcoal paint.

For a moment, the ghost rotates slowly, like a hanged corpse buffeted by the wind, and then it starts to move. I follow until it passes through the wall at the far end of the hallway and vanishes. Beyond the wall is only empty air and the drop to the frozen lake below.

* * *

Gertrude, the matron, has no qualms about taking me into her bed. She is a large, broad-shouldered woman, her silver hair always tightly coiled and braided whether she's on duty or off. The left side of her face is ruined, with a milky white eye sunken in a latticework of scars. When she was a junior nurse on the ward, she let down her guard while cleaning a cell in the catacombs and a patient clawed her from behind.

"Fuck me hard, Rattlecock," she says. I reach between my legs and my largest cock pops out like the corkscrew on a Swiss army knife. I know from experience this one is Gertrude's favorite. Gertrude throws me across the room and pummels me against the wall until I feel my chassis crack. This does not bother me; I know that the director will repair it easily. When she tires of the game, Gertrude leans over the vanity and I enter her from below. She is primed and our session is quick as it always is.

When we're done, Gertrude pulls a satchel of blue powder from her bedside drawer, pinches one nostril and inhales the powder in one long snort. Outside, the wind is howling and hail stones rattle the stained glass windows depicting the deaths of the saints.

"You seem distracted, Rattlecock."

"I saw something in the hallway."

Gertrude nods, still wiping her nose and snuffling loudly. “The bloody priest on the prowl, eh?”

“No. A woman. She looked like me.”

“A double, huh? That’s an ill omen.” Gertrude stands up and stretches. The tendons in her thick arms snap and pop. “The Germans say that seeing your double, your doppelganger as they call it, is a premonition of death. You seen this apparition before?”

“No.”

“Does the director know?”

“No.”

“I wouldn’t tell her then,” says Gertrude. “She’s got enough to worry about.” She pats me on my thigh. “And I enjoy these little sessions. We wouldn’t want to lose you.”

* * *

The director is waiting for me, lying naked upon our bed, when I return to the refectory. We once looked like twin sisters, because the director designed me to look like this, but time has dulled our similarities: Her hair is streaked with gray and her face has wrinkles at the corners of her eyes.

“You’re back. No problems?”

“No, Fraulein Director.”

The director reaches between my legs and changes my cock to a cunt. I have five cocks, but I have several cunts too. At night, the Turkish lamps make our room into a sweltering greenhouse.

“You seem distracted,” she says.

I don't tell her about the ghost. "I laid with Martha tonight."

The director tenses. "You do her more harm than good. But that's not your fault. This form displeases her, but you couldn't be any other way. It would be too dangerous to have a man stay at the asylum. You understand of course?"

"Yes, Fraulein Director."

"Every patient here suffers from dangerous hysteria and the musk of a man would send them into a carnal frenzy. No, for their own good, they must never be allowed to come near a man. But you, sister, you are the perfect form to help them. These soft breasts, these wide hips, your femininity repels them yet they are slaves to their baser urges… and they cannot resist."

Sometimes, when she gets excited, the director lets slip that word. *Sister*. The word excites me too.

The director's hand remains between my legs, her fingers sinking into the spongy flesh of my hidden lips. They are made of India rubber and quite realistic. I start to leak engine grease.

"You have the form of a woman, but you are what I made you: an automaton. I say this not to be cruel, but only so that you understand. No god ever laid down a prohibition against a machine. If Martha chooses to feel shame, that's her prerogative. But you have nothing to feel ashamed about. Do you understand?"

The director is correct, of course. My eyes are discs of cobalt blue glass. My skin is locking plates of porcelain, bone white and cold to the touch. My hair is horsehair. The director's hand massages my cunt until my breathing quickens and then her fingers slide inside me. My mouth finds mine and we fall into bed together.

The director laughs. "How silly of me. Sometimes I almost think it matters whether you understand."

She pushes the fingers of her free hand into my mouth.

* * *

The director is asleep, her chest rising and falling with her deep breathing. I don't sleep as people do, but I sometimes go quiet and stare at the wall and my mind goes elsewhere. When it returns, I find that hours have passed and that sometimes I return to reality with strange ideas in my head. I imagine this is what dreaming is like. This is how I realized the ghost could not be my double. A ghost is an echo of a person, but I am not a person.

But the director also looks like me.

I wait until the director starts to stir. She rolls over in bed and blinks blearily at me, a slow smile spreading across her face.

"You sleep well?"

"Yes."

"Good." She rises from bed and shrugs into a robe, pulling it tight around her waist. She leaves her breasts exposed as she toddles toward the stove and lights the fire.

"Last night, I saw a ghost."

"Ah. The bloody priest?"

"No. A woman. She looked like you."

The director puts down her tea and her papers. She turns and regards me.

"I heard that to see your double is an ill omen," I continue. "I thought I should tell you."

"That's a silly superstition, but you must always tell me everything." She grabs my hand and laces her fingers between mine. "We shouldn't keep secrets from one another. I'm glad you told me."

I am an automaton, but I feel for the director as I feel for no one else in the asylum. Our bond is unbreakable. I want to weep from how much I think I love her.

* * *

The director no longer pulls me into bed. She's upset at the ghost, it troubles her. I'm sure of it. What other explanation is there for her sudden coldness? The days are short and gray, the nights are long and dark. The nurses rely on me more than ever, but the director is now always asleep when I return to our room. I wish I hadn't said anything about the ghost.

One night, someone knocks at the door. No one has ever knocked at the door during the winter before, and the nurses are immediately in a disarray. The director herself has to answer.

"Open up in the name of the magistrate!" roars a deep voice.

The director pauses. "No men!" she yells. "No men!"

"Open the door!" repeats the voice. "It's freezing, open the damn door!"

The director hesitates but then she throws up

her arms in resignation and opens the door. There are two hussars. Their faces and uniforms are caked with frost. It must be an urgent delivery since it could not wait until Spring.

"I specifically told the magistrate that there were to be only female couriers," says the director and though her tone is level I can tell that she is very angry. Even now, I expect that the scent of the men may excite the patients. I will probably have to do extra rounds for the next few days.

"It was necessary," says the first hussar. He indicates a hunched heap of rags between them. "This thing can't be trusted with women."

He hands the director a wax-sealed envelope. The director breaks it open, scans the letter within, scribbles a signature, and hands it back.

"Take these two down to the kitchen and serve them some hot soup," says the director to Martha. To the hussars, she says: "You can leave it here."

The second hussar pulls the scarf from his face; his eyes are tearing, his nose is red and leaking from the cold. "Begging your pardon, we got strict orders: We don't leave til *this thing* is safely locked up."

The creature between them has its wrists and ankles shackled; a stained bag is pulled over its head.

"Very well," says the director. She motions for them to follow and she leads the hussars, and their charge, down the spiral stairs that lead to the catacombs. A while later, she returns with the hussars in tow. Only now do they accept the offer of soup.

Martha sits them at a table in the kitchen and ladles hot stew into a pair of bowls. I linger in the doorway to watch. I have never seen a man up close, although I understand that most of them have cocks similar to mine. The first hussar has a bristly mustache, the other does not.

"You should have seen that thing at the trial," says the mustached hussar, ladling soup into his mouth. "Just stood there grinning the whole time the magistrate read the offenses, until they had to put a bag over its head. They couldn't stand the eyes, that was the thing. Weird, glassy things. Nothing human behind them at all."

He looks at me. I wonder if my cobalt blue eyes give the same impression.

"So what is that?" he asks. "Some kind of puppet?"

"That's an automaton," says the director.

"Stop asking stupid questions," says the second hussar. Then he points at my crotch and asks: "Is that supposed to be a cock?"

"It looks weird," says the mustached hussar. "Why's it look like that?"

"Oh, I get it," says the other. "It's cut. See, there? It's made to look like it's cut. Here now, what you make that out of?"

"Pig bladder," says the director.

"Oh." The hussars fall silent. Their curiosities satiated, they return to their meals.

* * *

"I need you to visit a patient in the catacombs."

I have never visited the catacombs before. The director has told me that I must not go there. The women imprisoned in the catacombs are dangerous, such that locking them away from the world is a kindness.

I notice daguerreotypes, too, showing the pieces of its previous partners. The director slides them under the papers. "You will take the western stairs. At the terminus, continue down the western hall until you reach a cell with a little hatch in the door. The occupant will be your assignment tonight."

I wait for the director to tell me which nurse will accompany me as per policy, but she says nothing more. Eventually, she looks at me in annoyance and I understand that I am to go alone. I have lived here with the director for many years, I believe, sharing a room and a bed. How is it that I have not noticed, until this very moment, that she does not have a mole at all.

* * *

I descend the spiral stairway into the catacombs below the asylum, a network of tunnels carved into the limestone where the walls are always damp. I wonder, as I pass heavy barred doorways, which one of these patients was the one who ruined Gertrude's face so many years ago.

There is a cell at the end of the hallway. I open the small hatch set into the thick wooden door and stare into the darkness beyond.

"Hello," I say. My voice bounces back, distorted. There is a pause and then, somewhere in the darkness, a sound like heavy chains sliding over stone. "This will be your first session?" I ask.

Silence.

"It's very routine," I say. "For many patients, the problem is a build-up of menstrual blood in the womb. Female semen will turn venomous if not released through regular climax, but we can purge the fluid by manual stimulation. I have several settings and you can choose the one that pleases you most."

A thin, plaintiff voice that could belong either to a very old woman or a very young boy finally replies: "You're alone, right?"

For some reason, I don't want to answer but I do. "Yes."

"They never done that at Magdeburg. Always had at least two hussars, even when they just brung in th' bread and water. You seen what I done to them girls?"

I remember the daguerreotypes.

"Open the door," says the voice. "Open the door and come inside."

I could refuse, if I wanted to. But I know that the director would not assign me this task if there was any real danger. My pulse quickens, but I unlock the door and I step inside.

"Once I went to chapel," says the voice. In the dark, gnarled hands slide over my flanks, testing my resilience. "Some priest tried to dissuade me from a life o' sin. Everything's a sin, they say. But not this, eh? Not with a machine."

"No," I say. "Not with a machine."

Suddenly, the hands shove me and I fall to the floor, my head hitting the wet flagstones with a loud clunk. The creature is upon me. Its talons dig into the seams between my porcelain plates and it pries the shell from my belly. This is a new game, but I understand that my partners each have different needs. Now it scrapes against my guts but my steel undercarriage is too thick for its claws to penetrate. With a cry of fury, it attacks my groin and rips my crotch turret from its socket – my insides spill out in a rush.

"Fuck you!" shrieks the voice with a mindless fury that hits me like a slap. It's the words rather than the attack that make me realize this is not a game and it's only now that I think I ought to resist, ought to raise my fists to protect my life. But my arms feel so heavy now. The clawed hands continue to rip at my guts. I am lying in a spreading pool of my own grease, I can sense it flowing out of me.

* * *

When my mind returns, I am being pulled over rough-hewn floors and dumped into a pile. The world vaguely comes into focus and I realize I am in the refectory; I stare up at the familiar green and yellow Turkish lamps that dangle from the ceiling. The director is here, her face over mine. Her eyes are red. Her hands caress my face.

"It's broken," she says. "The stupid thing is broken."

I want to respond, but I don't have the will.

"I tried so hard to make you warm," says the director. "I wish I could have done more." She touches my forehead. "I tried so hard. If I could have just saved her memories, you would understand."

She is crying now. Her tears are different than

the ones shed by Martha, and they frighten me.

"I didn't know what to do. I didn't know what to do!" she cries. "Do you understand how much you frightened me?"

Sister. I cannot reply. I am choking on engine grease.

"We never left the Manor House, not after mother died. Father put us in the cellar. You don't remember the cellar, do you? My God, how can you not remember the cellar. If there was one memory of hers that I could have saved, it would have been that cellar. If you could remember that cellar, you would understand. We only had each other, didn't we?"

I think I am dying.

"But we escaped, didn't we? And we made something of our lives. It wasn't easy, but together... we could accomplish so much. But life was different when we were free from the cellar. Maybe the priest could turn a blind eye to our love when we were confined, maybe he could convince himself that god would forgive us for that, but did he think I would stop loving you when we were out in the world? Ridiculous. But he got in Magdalene's head that it was a sin. How could it be a sin? We loved each other as only sisters can. Now she's gone and there's just *you.*"

I am dying.

"It wasn't a sin with you, though," says the director. "It wasn't a sin with you because you're not a person. You're just a machine." Her sobs rattle inside her chest and her breath comes in ragged gasps. "But you're not her. I wish I had given you a name. But I couldn't."

She pounds her fists on my chassis. Cracks spiderweb through my skin.

"You're not her. You're not her at all." Suddenly her despair turns to anger. "Fuck you! Fuck you! Fuck you!"

Her fury is worse than the creature in the catacombs because she is the director, she is my sister, and I cannot imagine her angry. She loves me.

She shoves me over the edge of the table and I fall to the ground with a clatter. Whatever the creature in the catacombs has begun is being completed now.

"You saw her in the hallway. You didn't even know it was her. How could you know anything? That she would show herself to YOU and stay hidden from me, all these years…" She kicks at me. "Fuck you! Fuck you! Fuck you!"

Gertrude was correct. To see your double is indeed an omen of death.

Outside, the wind rattles the windows and the splintered shingles of the rooftops. The snow starts to fall again.

PA(I)NCAKES

Dex Drury

Flip
of my stomach when you spoon me half-naked
sternum to spine, bleeding my pink-tinted batter
into the heart-shaped riddle, "Are you queer?"
like debating cinnamon or vanilla
when I know both give me hives

Flop
into a hot heartfelt confession rejection griddle
spatula straight, you scrape at my soft belly
turn its bubbled top and slap me down
my pining hopes for a morning-after breakfast
pop crisp to a bitter burnt brown

Flap
me on a stack of steaming leftover victims
of fluffy "maybe-more-than-friends" flirtation
victims squeezed into one single-use plastic bag
we wither in your ice box, crystallizing stiff
passionate love professions preserved to please you

Jack
up the heat when you're hungry so our unrequited
unease softens below defrost, tongue teasing
lamentations that we were born incompatible genders
words wrong-sticky like the high-fructose fake shit
no authentic maple grade gay fancy syrup
to soothe smitten microwave-nuked surrenders

Blap
as you dollop past whims with whipped scream profanity
slice of knife and fork stabs in ossified sides
you chew off the freezer burn-fused edges of our affections
roll us into a bolus and ingest our silly infatuations
to satiate your insecure vanities

Snap
our heartbreak packs your cavities
with rotted "can't-move-on" carrion tenacity
our devotion disintegrates in gastric acid
as you giggle at the next simp to succumb
flashing the gnashing crush of your butter greased gums

EAT YOUR HEART OUT

Mason Hawthorne

A cockatoo glows white against the greenish shadows of the trees. It turns its head back and forth, beady black eyes narrowed, yellow crest fanning up and down as it paces across the grass and leaf litter.

The sun is hot across his back, and cold mud wets his cheek, soaks through his good button-down, and weekend jeans. He forces his eyes open, and the world is a dazzling smear; the sight of the cockatoo burns so bright it hurts his head. He grunts and rests his forehead against a tussock of grass dewed with blood.

Diesel exhaust hangs thick in the air, and the world spins. There's no breeze, and the only sounds are the tick-tick-tick of cooling metal, and his own ragged breathing. He could sleep. His eyes are heavy and the sun's heat lulls him. His stomach growls. He wants to ignore it, just close his eyes and rest. But the cockatoo moves closer, its jagged beak opening and closing. He has seen them chew through tree branches and power lines; a finger would be no challenge.

Dizzy, stomach gurgling, he flops onto his side, facing the ute, which is wrapped around an old tree stump, the engine mashed into a V-shape, and the windscreen exploded. Squares of safety glass press into his palm. A tickle on his cheek; he wipes his face with the back of his hand and it comes away red. His stomach churns. He looks at the ute again, at the driver's door flung open, smeared with blood, then back to the blood on his arm.

Lurching onto his knees, he's sick, heaving until tears stream down his face and his nose runs. He tastes the bitter backwash of white wine and canapés. He staggers up, takes a few tottering steps and falls again, landing amidst a dense clump of white arum lilies. Fleshy petals press against his cheek, and cold water soaks through his jeans. A rush of wings sounds behind him, the cockatoo flies close overhead and lands on the crumpled hood of the ute. It eyes him, then lifts one claw to scratch around its beak, beady black eyes trained on him.

A sob catches in his chest, he presses a hand against his stomach.

Nick? It's Joseph's voice, soft and close by his ear. *Nicky? Where are you?*

"Joseph?" It comes out reedy, thin and weak in the hot sunlight. Nick turns to look at the ute, at the closed passenger door, at the windscreen busted out from that side. "Joseph? Oh god, oh fuck, Joseph!"

Nick, help me! He sounds afraid, his deep voice cracking as it bottoms out.

Nick pushes himself upright, the lilies' thick stems crushing under his hands. A bright pain arcs along his arm as the stinging nettles growing between the flowers swipe against his skin. "Shit, shit, shit!"

Nick, please! Help!

"Where are you, Joseph?"

Always Joseph, never Joe, was how he was introduced. They were at some party in the city, Nick feeling out of place in his new shirt and shoes, sweating because he didn't know how to talk about art, and he'd never before drunk wine that wasn't out of a goon sack.

"Where are you?"

He trips over his own feet and the broken lily stems as he turns. He's in a shallow drainage ditch along the side of the road. A barbed wire fence runs alongside that, and beyond is a stand of scrubby trees, a cool and shady island in the middle of a wide, rolling grassy field.

"Joseph?"

Nick turns to look behind himself, but the dirt road is empty; the ditch glitters with broken glass and shallow water, the grass is darkly smeared with his own blood.

Turn around, Nicky, please help me, please!

Joseph's voice sounds close, as though he's speaking directly into Nick's ear. He turns again, back towards the trees. The cockatoo, still on the ute, stretches its neck up and turns as well, its yellow crest on full display.

Something is crumpled at the base of a thick-trunked flame tree, in the dappled shade of the tree-line. Nick's eyes water, and he has to blink hard and squint before he's sure of what he's looking at.

"Fuck." Nick staggers to the barbed wire fence. Bending to hold the strands so that he can pass through it, he wobbles on his feet. His good shirt snags on a barb, and he catches the back of his head on the top wire. More blood.

In the shadows under the flame tree's glossy dark green canopy, Joseph looks like he could be sleeping. From a distance. Sitting propped against the trunk, his chin on his chest, arms splayed limply at his sides, spread-eagled. If it weren't for the star-shaped gouge across his forehead, or the line of blood running from his ear.

Nick falls to his hands and knees, and crawls to Joseph, reaches to grasp his foot and shake it, but there is no response. Joseph is still, his face slack. His grey eyes are open, glazed and fixed. A fly loops through the still air, circles, and lands at the corner of Joseph's open mouth, rubbing its little forelegs together before it begins probing into the darkness between his lips.

"No," Nick says, he moves closer, waves the fly away from Joseph's face. "Joseph," he says, pressing his shoulders, and then catching up one of his soft, long-fingered hands, "Joseph?"

Nothing. And then, as though Joseph's lips are pressed against Nick's ear.

Help me, Nicky.

"Help you what? Joseph, I can't…I don't…"

Joseph's fine, flyaway hair is plastered to his forehead with blood, his tanned skin ashen. He's tall but fine-boned, but now he looks like a doll version of himself, shrunken and disjointed. If it weren't for the blood, he could be sleeping, and he looks so much like the child that Nick has seen in school photographs, in the framed pictures Joseph's mother keeps on her walls that Nick makes a strangled, animal noise and squeezes his still-warm lifeless hand, leans forward and mashes his lips to Joseph's slack mouth.

Nick, help me.

"I can't—I'll—" *call Dad*, is what he is about to say. I'll call Dad, he'll know what to do. Nick's dad who has always been solid, dependable. Practical. Who'd treated Nick's coming out with the same equanimity as he did an unexpected storm, or a good season. Who had made a point of favouring Joseph, at the big family Christmas dinner, had offered to teach him to shoot, or ride a horse, while Nick's sister's boyfriend-du-jour stewed with resentment.

Dad won't be able to fix this one.

Don't leave me here, Nick.

"The ute's fucked, I can't carry you back. I can't even stand straight."

Don't leave me alone. I can hear them, the—

Wings clatter through the air overhead, a flash of white. The cockatoo settles onto one of the flame tree's lower branches, the feathers around its neck puffed up, the yellow crest rising and falling. It bobs its head and opens its razor beak to screech. Nick crumples, ears ringing. He grips Joseph's shoulder for balance.

Don't let them get me, Nick, don't leave me here to rot!

"I have to get help," Nick says, "I'll call an ambulance, or something, I have to…to get help. I have to get help."

Nick, you have to help me, don't leave me, don't leave me here Nick.

"I can't help you alone."

Nick, you need to help me, you did this to me! Don't leave me here to rot as well!

"I didn't…I didn't, it was an accident." His throat is dry and the words curl on his tongue like dead leaves.

They're coming for me, Nick. They're going to chew me into pieces and I'm going to rot here. Worms, Nick, I'm wormfood. Maggots.

"Oh shit, Joseph, no, no," Nick wants to cover his ears but the voice is so close, like they're whispering together with their heads on the same pillow, "Joseph, no, no." His face is wet again, tears mingling with the blood that is starting to dry, making it run and drip down to patter across Joseph's white jeans.

There's worse than maggots, Nicky, I can hear them coming for me, flying right to me. They want to eat me up, Nick, they want to pull me to pieces, and it'll hurt, Nick, it'll hurt the whole time.

"No, Joseph, baby," Nick's voice breaks, hitches with each breath, "you're dead, angels are s'posed to come and take you off to heaven. It's supposed to be nice."

It isn't nice here, Nick. It's dark, and it's hungry. And I'm scared.

"I'll try, I'll try to carry you. To the road, at least. If we can get there, then someone will find us. I…I think I can get you that far." In the quiet under the trees, the hum of insects grows more distinct. Small, black flies circle around them. When they try to land on Joseph's face, Nick waves them away. Something tickles along Nick's forehead, he wipes his face, hisses as his finger catches the gash over his temple. His hand comes away sticky.

There's nowhere you can take me where I'll be safe.

Joseph's voice is so close by Nick's ear that he

can feel the stir of the small hairs on the back of his neck, like Joseph's breath on him. He shivers, and looks up. The cockatoo is still watching them, head bobbing like it can hear a rhythm, its black eyes sharp.

"What can I do, then?" Nick wards another fly away and a wave of dizziness rocks him.

You're the only one who can help me now, Nick.

"Tell me what to do."

You won't like it, but it's the only way.

"Tell me."

You have to eat me first.

Nick jerks as though he's been hit, his face burns and his teeth clench. Overhead the cockatoo lets out a long, low shriek.

You have to, Nicky, my love. You have to eat me before they do.

"No," Nick shakes his head, sweat beads along his upper lip. His stomach growls.

Don't argue, Nick. You did this to me. You did this. Where's that knife you've always got on you? Take it out.

Nick's fingers fumble over the leather pouch on his belt, his fingernail bends backwards before he manages to pry the snaps open. The knife fits in the palm of his hand, folded so that the blade is hidden in the handle. *Ooh*, Joseph used to say, *you're so butch, aren't you? You really carry that everywhere you go?* And Nick had blushed and mumbled something like *well, you never know when you'll need to slice an apple.* Now there is none of that sweet teasing in Joseph's voice. It is flat, and fearful.

"I didn't mean to," Nick says with numb lips.

He was driving too fast. They'd had a couple of drinks and lunch had gone longer than they'd intended, and they needed to get back so they wouldn't be late for…well it hardly matters now. "I didn't mean to."

I know. Open it. Here, let me help. Let me hold your hand. Don't be scared.

Nick presses the button and unfolds the blade. There's a tickle on the back of his hand, and then the suggestion of a sensation, as though Joseph's soft hands are wrapped around his wrists, but faint, cool. Joseph's hands are limp at his sides, pale among the leaf litter. Nick allows his hand, holding the knife, to be guided up, to slice open Joseph's shirt and reveal the soft stretch of his belly, the wispy tuft of pale hair at his breastbone.

"I can't do this," Nick whispers.

Close your eyes, don't be scared. Nothing you do can hurt me now. I need you to help me.

The knife is light, and warm from his body heat. And Nick does close his eyes, but that only means that he feels all the more clearly as the blade snags something firm and supple and giving, the pressure as it is drawn down through the layers of skin, and fat, and muscle, the grate of it nicking bone. He shudders, his hand sweats and the handle is slippery in his palm. He opens his eyes to entrails, pink and red and green and yellow, and still warm.

"I can't do this," he's shaking, his breath hitching in half-sobs.

You'd do it if you loved me.

It's like a slap, Nick recoils. "How can you say that? Of course, I love you. I love you!" He's crying, fat tears dribbling down his cheeks.

Help me, Nick. Don't be scared. You've done this before, you big tough country boy.

He's done this before, with rabbits and pigs, and a goat. Gutted fish by the river to carry home for Dad to cook on the barbie with thyme fresh from the garden. What is blood? What are guts? Nothing; just waste material, just the stuff you've got to be careful with so you don't spoil the meat. Nick pushes a hand into the mass of intestine and carefully lifts it, pulling and turning so that it will come free. He turns the knife aside, the last thing he wants is to puncture the bowels, to contaminate everything.

Just a bit more, Nicky, you're nearly there.

The intestines spill out onto the soil, and Nick pushes his hand into the cavity, reaches up and slices through the diaphragm. Clotting blood sluices out, splashes onto his lap, his good shirt. Nick grits his teeth and pushes his fingers up, between the lungs, through to the rubbery protective sack around the heart. It is like picking fruit, plucking a ripe orange from the tree. It is heavy in his hand, warm from the sun.

Nick sways where he kneels and draws his hand out, holding it carefully, overripe fruit which his fingers will bruise. He sniffles, sucks in a deep breath around the surges of panic that constrict his chest, squeeze him. The hand on his wrist, the hand that isn't there, guides his hand up to his mouth, and the gamey, metallic smell of blood hits him, fresh blood, thickening in the heat of the day.

You've got to do it, Nick, now. Please.

"I love you Joseph," Nick says, "I'm sorry for

what I did."

I love you too, Nick. You're making it right. I love you.

Nick lifts his hand the last little way by himself, and bites deep.

Overhead, the cockatoo lets out a final screech, and hurtles up, out of the canopy of the flame tree and into the wide blue cloudless sky.

THEY CALL THAT

Avi Ben-Zeev

Hey Amos, remember me talking your furry ear off about Pema Chodron?

No? Nothing?

This tidbit should help—Pema's the Zen Buddhist nun who threw a stone at her cheating husband before turning into a spiritual warrior in 1981. Fierce, right, my Amos? I can't imagine any public figure admitting to throwing stones in 2051, Red or Blue.

Anyway, Pema tells a riveting story about what we call things. I know, I know, riveting and labels; sounds like an oxymoron, but care to hear the story anyway?

And don't think I don't see it—how you yawn and stretch your brindle body in the flying taxi pod. You don't care about spirituality or enlightenment, do you, my sweet dog? I feel your pain. It's not easy being trapped in bumper-to-bumper air traffic, not even with a bird's eye view of the Golden Gate Bridge.

Pema's story should help with claustrophobia. There's no sex or violence, but it's a good story. I promise you, my Amos. And if I get it wrong, please don't hold it against me.

It's 4 a.m. I'm in bed, not in a taxi, traversing

the twilight between wakefulness and sleep, and you are dead.

* * *

Right. Pema's story.

Once upon a time, in a land far, far away, there were two monks. Their favorite pastime was meditating, side-by-side, for hours on end. Enlightenment or the ultimate escapism? Whichever, one sunny day, sitting cross-legged at the foot of a blossoming Elm, the senior monk spoke out loud, breaking the order's vow of silence.

"They call that … a *tree*!" the elder said, and at the exclamation, the friends brayed so hard they pissed their pants.

Aw, my beloved Amos, you'd be tilting your head, puzzled at the happy noises I'm finally making. Allow me to explain. I'm not condescending, I promise; it took me a while before I went—*Ah*! You see, a tree is so much more nuanced and complex than its label; at least, that's what I think the moral is.

And it stuck with me because when I come out as a trans man—*they* call *me* a … what exactly?

And by *they*, I mean the bearish nonbinaries I've been dating. And by dating, I mean Virtual Reality sex or interview-style back-and-forths that leave me lonelier than being solo.

Still, my bed is empty, my Amos, and my heart? It wants a lover I could wake up to In Real Life and smile, even if they farted under the covers or didn't clean themselves well, so the smell of their shit still lingered on my bionic prosthetic dick.

I confess. A week ago, I ventured into the musty book archives—yes, they've become obsolete, but some retro renegades are keeping them going—for a yellowing copy of *If The Buddha Dated.*

Would the Buddha have, though?

Whatever the answer, I inhaled the pages, filling my lungs with that earthy aroma. I'm sorry I yelled at you, my Amos, for chewing up *Enormous Changes at the Last Minute*. I get it now—decomposition's irresistible fragrance, a reminder that life is fleeting, however extended.

* * *

I miss cuddling you—the real you, not a tactile facsimile that's somehow too crisp, too perfect, no matter how much I try weakening its settings. It kills me you guys live for such a short time.

When will death be cured? Will it?

Earlier today, I did something reckless or brave; you decide. I joined a private VR dating group: Gay Trans Men 4 Gay Trans Men. I'll tell you later how I found out it existed, but for now, I'll say this—it took jumping hoops to get in.

The first thing I did was skim the profiles. Two hundred members and counting. Most were from Blue cities, like San Francisco and New York. Blue or Red, we were all incognito—moderator's rules.

When I stumbled on Cub, I paused. There was something about his writing—a sorrow tinged with hope that broke my heart.

`How about a movie date later tonight?` I messaged.

Cub replied right away. Appreciate the offer, but you're catching me at a bad time. I was just about to deactivate my profile.

That's a shame. My intuition says that we'd like each other. Persisting might have been foolish, but what was the point of trying to connect if I didn't say how I felt?

You know what? I could use the distraction, Cub wrote.

His change of heart wasn't flattering, exactly, but I liked his honesty. Besides, fictitious or not, Cub's pic was cute—hipster beard, round belly, and spectacles circa the 1980s.

* * *

Half an hour before the date was slated to start, my hands got sticky, and a pebble lodged in my throat. I wanted to meet someone like me, whatever that meant, but I was scared, terrified even. You got this, I told myself. Freaking out could wait.

Tactile suit settings? Check.

Goggles connected? Check.

Ready or not, I logged in.

How embarrassing to be so early and thirsty, but guess what? Cub was already in our private theater, pacing back and forth. Conscientious and neurotic meets conscientious and neurotic—romantic, don't you think?

"I admit, I have a thing for gingers, but what do you look like In Real Life?" Cub asked.

"IRL? Pretty much like my avatar—athletic, tattooed, okay, perhaps an inch shorter and younger.

Think mid-40s not early-50s."

Cub laughed. "A trans-Muppet?"

"Oops. I'm ashamed to admit it, but I went to this Jim Henson sing-along tribute, and I guess I forgot to change my face." Outing myself as a Muppet Show fan meant my street cred was shot. Never mind, a few quick touches, and voila, replacing Animal's thick eyebrows and shaggy, red hair with the face I saw when I looked in the mirror—there was my avatar twin, wearing a flannel shirt, black jeans and baseball cap.

"A trucker? Wow, quite the subversive outfit," Cub exclaimed.

"Don't get me wrong, I know how lucky I am to live in the post-gender bubble that's San Francisco—and I love the proliferation of non-binary identities, really I do, but it's a relief just to be—"

"Your binary self? Believe me, I get it."

I've been dreaming of being seen, my Amos, so what sharpened the pain in my chest? "To be honest, I feel shame about being a double binary. A gay transguy, as though one weren't enough."

Cub's lip curled. "So, you're buying into the Blue everyone-is-nonbinary dogma?"

"What? No. It's just that—"

"I'm sick of it all." Cub's face reddened as though we were IRL. "Reds persecuting us. Blues social policing us out of existence." His voice was loud and shrill.

Cub's reaction was intense, my Amos, but I heard him about the Reds. Just this morning at the Federal Gender Clinic, the nurse told me that unless I checked the heterosexual box from now on, the government would take me off their bionic-prosthetic upgrades list. "No more testosterone either," the nurse said.

But the Blues? I resonate with their post-gender values. The label "man" is so fucking loaded with privilege and misogyny, and I hate it; I really do, so why, when I close my eyes, do I feel like a man? Is there something wrong with me, my Amos?

"I'm sorry I raised my voice; it's been an overwhelming week." Cub sat on the double leather recliner, facing the screen. "Are you still up for watching a movie? I'm dying to see the new Bond flick."

"Sure," I said. Cub's outburst didn't feel good, but I sensed a longing beneath his anger—a universal desire to belong. And I wished for Cub, no, I wished for us, to live and love freely.

As I sat beside him, our thighs touched, and I gasped like a schoolboy. What would it be like to have sex with another trans man? Do our identities, our IRL bodies, even matter in Virtual Reality?

Overthinking, as usual, I reached for the touch screen. "Show time," I said, pressing *Bond 50.* Then, leaning back, I surrendered to not knowing, or at least I tried, the double recliner molding itself to our shapes, floating in space.

* * *

There's nothing like losing myself in a volumetric film, my sweet Amos, gorging popcorn doused in fake butter, an iced Coke's fizziness tingling my tongue, and, of course, there was Bond—Foxy Brown in holographic realness. Hello.

But something wasn't quite right with Cub. Halfway through the movie, he kept tap, tap, tapping his fingers on my thigh, and I should have said something, but I didn't want to offend him.

Cub's finger drumming got more and more irritating. Imagine the climactic scene—infallible Pam Grier maneuvering wildly to save humanity, and all I wanted to do was scream. *Stop it!*

Finally, the credits rolled, and I couldn't wait to say goodbye, but Cub stalled. "There's something I'm dying to get off my chest." His avatar lowered its chin and raised its eyes, pup-like. "Okay, if we meet IRL?"

"In Real Life?" I echoed, parrot-like. "No, I only meet IRL if—"

"I wouldn't ask if it wasn't important. Trust me, gay trans man to gay trans man." Cub nodded his head as if he needed me to agree. "Yerba Buena Gardens? The park's empty, except for the houseless, of course."

Late-night IRL dates with strangers are risky, I know you know, my Amos, but something in my gut told me to relent. "Okay, my pod ride should only take about fifteen minutes."

Cub placed his hand on his chest. "Great, see you in fifteen by the MLK memorial."

"Wait, how will I recognize you?"

"I'll be the only one with glasses," he said and vanished, leaving me with a half-eaten bag of popcorn and a sugary, salty taste on my tongue.

* * *

My taxi landed on the empty lot facing the park's entrance. Stepping outside, I braced myself for a coughing fit—the hazardous smoke particles in the Bay Area had been in the news again—but my filtration mask did the trick.

It was hot, but not too hot, so I turned off the temperature controls on my jumpsuit and headed to the meeting point. Remember, Amos, how once upon a time we went for nightly strolls, maskless, and there were trees for you to sniff and pee on? Now, there's endless concrete, but when I close my eyes, I can still smell blossoms and picture you wagging your body, tail to head, ears back, smiling.

Nostalgia put a spring in my step, or maybe it was the promise of romance, however improbable, or the sky, darker than a city normally allowed, or the stars shining iridescent light on Martin Luther King's memorial—a giant waterfall spilling and roaring over granite. And I know, I know, optimism is a tricky beast, but why not dream in dreamlike realness?

"Hi, gorgeous." Cub startled me from behind. He was taller and thinner than I had expected, about 6 feet—more otter-like than bearish—with a gaunt face and chiseled chin. And, yes, he had frames on with no lenses, so it must have been him.

"Hi, Cub." I wanted to add something kind or witty, but my IRL etiquette was rusty.

"Thanks for meeting me here." Cub removed his mask and motioned for me to join him on a bench. Up close, the purple, red, and brown patches on his cheeks and neck looked familiar. Where had I seen these before?

Light-headed, I gazed at the vastness above. In

Real Life looked like a movie but grainier. "There's still beauty left in this world," I said.

"You're the most beautiful thing here." Cub must have caught onto my *ugh*-face and shook his head, "Sorry, that was corny."

"More like trying too hard," I injected playfulness into my tone.

We laughed, and the naked human under the lunar-powered lamppost, cleaning their pubic hair with a tiny comb, cracked a toothless smile. There are three billion houseless in this living-dying world. Can you believe it, my Amos?

"It's been a hell of a week. I've been sleeping a lot and waking into nightmares." Cub stared at his hands. "But being IRL with you makes all the difference."

"What happened?" I asked. If the Buddha dated, I'd venture the Buddha would have made a polite excuse and left, and I almost did, my Amos, but cheesy and all, *they* call *us … wrong.*

Cub sighed. "I got diagnosed with AIDS. Not HIV, but AIDS. Full-blown AIDS."

* * *

AIDS, my Amos? I couldn't believe it. It's 2051, not 1991, the year Lou Sullivan died because AZT proved ineffective. Wasn't HIV/AIDS eradicated in 2030, for goodness' sake?

I told you about Lou. Remember, Amos? He's my hero—the first out and proud gay trans man in San Francisco, no, the world. The gender clinics refused to Lou gender-affirming care because people like us, trans men who loved men, weren't supposed to exist. You see—so-called misfits and deviants had othering labels, but unreal others had no labels.

Here's the thing about Lou—he rang the gender clinics, refusing invisibility or silence. "You told me I couldn't live as a gay man, but it looks like I'm going to die like one." How heartbreaking that it took a deadly disease to affirm Lou's identity. Now, sixty years later, my Amos and some of *us* are still *them* on the social hierarchy, outside and within our communities, whatever community means.

* * *

"You seem lost in thought." Cub touched my arm. "Did I scare you off?"

"Must be shocking." What else could I have said?

"It's a new variant of HIV/AIDS. Even more aggressive than in the eighties." Cub coughed into a handkerchief, bloodying the white linen. "They're infecting us."

"What?" Did he say what I thought he did?

"That's why I wanted to meet you here. I needed to warn you without risking anyone listening in." Cub's stare was raw, a nakedness I had never witnessed.

"What *they* are you talking about? Who is doing this?" I wiped the sweat off my forehead and pressed my jumpsuit's cooling function.

"Hold me? I don't have much time left." Cub inched closer.

Enveloping his trembling body, my mind

flashed to documentaries of New York City at the epidemic's height—gay men dying on street benches, skin-and-bones, colorful Kaposi Sarcoma tumors spreading over their skin and into their lungs.

I wanted to comfort Cub, my Amos; I honestly did, but how? Stay present or repress and deny? There was no manual.

In the end, it wasn't a matter of conjuring the right words. Cub cried softly into my chest, and in holding him, I held myself, the phantom of your chin resting on my knee.

They call that...

tree,
trans,
tumor,
2051,
1984.

too much

Lor Gislason

My first love barely let me touch her
except for stolen kisses in bathroom stalls
and my fingers brushing her Rapunzel hair

I never saw her naked.

My second, as if to make up for lost time,
I showered in affection; my mouth everywhere
because I could. Because she let me.
Eventually, I became Too Much.

To the third, I was a spare, a backup
You're cute, but not beautiful, she told me
and a piece of me I didn't know existed
shattered.

My fourth promised to show me stars,
my need to touch became obsession–
to make them stay, just a little while longer
It scarcely dried before the engine revved

Next time, they'd tell me,
you'll know heaven.

But the day never came

and neither did I.

By the fifth, I realized —
I was waiting for something

I didn't know if I wanted, anymore

or if it even existed in the first place.

By now, I realized, it wasn't that I didn't *want*
but that the pieces
                    didn't fit together
            as they should
An end never meeting a middle,
our edges grating.

Someday, maybe
I'll sand down those edges
until you want me again.

Author Biographies

Avi Ben-Zeev is a gay transgender man, high school failure, and Yale Ph.D. A psychologist and writer, he's compelled by emotional truth. His story *Angel* won the 2023 UK's first transgender writing prize, and his anthology *Trans Homo ... Gasp!* was a Lambda Award finalist. Find more at avibenzeev.com

Elizabeth Lynn Blackson grew up in a small town in Eastern Ohio, living on a steady diet of comic books, horror movies, and Stephen King novels, while playing D&D and listening to heavy metal. It twisted her into the maniacal creature you now see before you. While certain she was going to be a comic artist, life pulled her in a different direction, and she ended up in the St. Louis metro area, where she lives with her hubby and two cats.

Amanda Nevada DeMel is an emerging speculative fiction author. Her favorite genre is horror, thanks to careful cultivation from her father. She especially appreciates media that can simultaneously scare her and make her cry. Additionally, she loves reptiles, musicals, and breakfast foods.

Minh-Anh Vo Dinh is a queer Vietnamese horror screenwriter in Toronto and an alum of the Canadian Film Centre's Writers Lab 2023. He likes unsettle and spook audiences with a focus on queer and female Asian voices, believing that their unique perspectives can elevate the genre with nuances. His queer horror short story *I Wander The Earth Longing to Taste Your Beating Heart* is a part of *The Pleasure In Pain: A Queer Horrotica Anthology* by Dragon's Roost Press (April 2024). On top of that, he is currently developing his Vietnamese folk horror feature *The Other* with a production company.

Phillip E. Dixon is an English Professor from Las Vegas whose fiction has appeared in *Cosmic Horror Monthly*, *The Fabulist*, *After Dinner Conversation*, and elsewhere. He holds an MFA in Writing from Lindenwood University, drinks his coffee black, and collects Transformers toys like a proper middle-aged nerd.

Dex Drury writes transgressive poetry packed with an abundance of rhyme, rainbows, and fluffy horror metaphor.

Mason Hawthorne studied creative writing at the University of Wollongong, and has stories in Midnight Echo Magazine, *Unspeakable: a Queer Gothic Anthology*, *The Monsters we Forgot* anthology and *Kaleidoscope: A Queer Anthology 2023*.
Twitter: @MasonHawth0rne
Bluesky: @masonhawthorne.bsky.social
Tumblr: @masonhawth0rne

Lor Gislason (they/he) is a non-binary homebody from Vancouver Island, Canada. With a focus on body horror, their work has been featured in *Escalators to Hell: Shopping Mall Horrors, Ooze: Little Bursts of Body Horror* and *Sick! Stories from the Goop Troop.* They live with their partner and two cats, Pastel and Pierogi Platter.

Anastasia Jill (they/them, ze/hir) is a queer writer living in Central Florida. They have been nominated for Best American Short Stories, The Pushcart Prize, and several other honors. Their work has been featured or is upcoming with *Poets.org, Sundog Lit, Flash Fiction Online, Contemporary Verse 2, Broken Pencil,* and more.

Bitter Karella (He/him, She/her) is a genderfluid writer and proprictor of the microfiction comedy account @Midnight_Pals. When not writing, she dabbles in cartooning and text game design. Twitter/Tumblr/Bluesky/Mastodon: bitterkarella

Lindsay King-Miller is the author of *Ask a Queer Chick: A Guide to Sex, Love, and Life for Girls who Dig Girls* (Plume, 2016) and *The Z Word* (Quirk, 2024). Her fiction has appeared in Fireside Fiction, Baffling Magazine, and numerous other publications. Her second novel *This Is My Body* is forthcoming from Quirk Books in 2025. She lives in Denver, CO with her partner and their two children.

Norah Lovelock (they/she) is a queer vegetarian from

the north of England. Her fiction has appeared in *Metaphorosis* and is forthcoming in *Planet Scumm.* They live with their cat, who occasionally permits them outside for enrichment and exercise. You can find her online at https://norah.love

Avra Margariti is a queer author, Greek sea monster, and Rhysling-nominated poet with a fondness for the dark and the darling. Avra's work haunts publications such as *Vastarien*, *Asimov's*, and *F&SF*. *The Saint of Witches*, Avra's debut collection of horror poetry, is available from Weasel Press. You can find Avra on twitter @avramargariti

Marisca Pichette is a queer author based in Massachusetts, on Pocumtuck and Abenaki land. Her work has appeared in *Strange Horizons, Clarkesworld, Vastarien, The Magazine of Fantasy & Science Fiction, Fantasy Magazine, Flash Fiction Online, Nightmare Magazine,* and others. Her speculative poetry collection, *Rivers in Your Skin, Sirens in Your Hair*, is out now from Android Press. Find them on Twitter as @MariscaPichette, Instagram as @marisca_write, and Bluesky as @marisca.bsky.social.

Eric Raglin (he/him) is a queer Nebraskan horror/Weird fiction writer. His short story collections include *Nightmare Yearnings*, *Extinction Hymns* (published by Brigids Gate Press), and *Lonesome Pyres* (forthcoming in 2024 through Off Limits Pulp). He owns Cursed Morsels Press and has edited *No Trouble at All* (with Alexis DuBon), *Bitter Apples*,

Shredded: A Sports and Fitness Body Horror Anthology, and *Antifa Splatterpunk*. Find him on Twitter, Bluesky, or Instagram @ericraglin1992.

Climber, tattoo collector, and peanut-butter connoisseur, **Xan van Rooyen** is an autistic, non-binary storyteller from South Africa, currently living in Finland where the heavy metal is soothing and the cold, dark forests inspiring. You can find Xan's stories in the likes of *Three-Lobed Burning Eye*, *Daily Science Fiction*, and *Galaxy's Edge* among others, as well as several novels including YA fantasy *My Name is Magic*, and adult arcanepunk novel *Silver Helix*. Xan is also part of the Sauutiverse, an African writer's collective with their first anthology *Mothersound* out now from Android Press.

Eva Roslin writes dark fantasy and historical horror. She is a Canadian writer of Armenian descent. An SFWA member, her works have appeared in publications that include: *Literally Dead: a Halloween anthology* (Alienhead Press), *Love Letters to Poe, Volume II: Houses of Usher* (ed. Sara Crocoll Smith), *Under Her Skin* (Black Spot Books), and others. She works as a librarian and researcher.

Marc Ruvolo (he/him) is a queer writer and musician living in Portland, Oregon who once considered himself a punk. He founded the seminal Bucket O' Blood book store in Chicago. His poetry and fiction have appeared in Cynthia Pelayo's *Gothic Blue Book* series, *The Night's End* horror podcast, and many others. A debut horror novella, *Sloe*, was released in

August 2023 by Unnerving Books. A second horror novella, *Pieties*, is available now from Off Limits Press. Find him on Twitter at @RuvFur and Bluesky @marcruvolo.bsky.social

Alan Mark Tong is a queer neurodivergent Chinese American writer of speculative fiction, although he sometimes ventures out into other genres. This is his first publication. He lives in Washington State with one spouse, two children, and two spoiled dogs. Follow him on Twitter @alanmarktong and on Bluesky @alanmarktong.bsky.social

Ezra Wu writes, draws, and very occasionally codes. They are non-binary and transmasc, and a lover of all things liminal. Get in touch via mastodon at @nebulos@comicscamp.club or check out their site at https://nebulos.space

Jamie Zaccaria is a wildlife conservationist by trade and writer by pleasure. She currently works for an ocean exploration organization and writes fiction in her spare time. Her anthology collection of short stories, *Lavender Speculation*, was released by Wildling Press in 2023. For a complete portfolio, please visit jamiezaccaria.com

Trigger Warnings

The following list is not exhaustive, but it takes into account certain themes and situations included in *Slay and Slay Again!*

- Assault (sexual & non-sexual)
- Blood / gore
- Cannibalism
- Death / loss of a partner
- Decomposition
- Domestic violence
- Dysphoria
- Gun violence
- HIV/AIDS crisis
- Homophobia
- Incest
- Mental health issues
- Sex
- Suicide
- Surgery / regret
- Transphobia

Made in United States
North Haven, CT
09 April 2025